Sure Shot . . .

Clint checked the bodies to make sure they were dead. Then he checked the man he had hit—Kemper—and was surprised to find two bullets in his chest. He wondered about that until he realized from the position the body was in, given where Bridget had been lying on the floor when she was shooting, it had to be she who had shot and killed him.

He wasn't sure whether he was going to tell her that or not.

The bartender came over to him and said, "These fellers were sayin' you probably killed the Lane brothers. Is that true?"

"It's true."

"Well then, friend," the barman said, "you just did Council Bluffs a service."

THE GUNSMITH

376

TRAIL TO SHASTA

J. R. ROBERTS

JOVE BOOKS, NEW YORK

THE BERKLEY PUBLISHING GROUP
Published by the Penguin Group
Penguin Group (USA) Inc.
375 Hudson Street, New York, New York 10014, USA

USA / Canada / UK / Ireland / Australia / New Zealand / India / South Africa / China

Penguin Books Ltd., Registered Offices: 80 Strand, London WC2R 0RL, England
For more information about the Penguin Group visit penguin.com

TRAIL TO SHASTA

A Jove Book / published by arrangement with the author

Jove Books are published by The Berkley Publishing Group.
JOVE® is a registered trademark of Penguin Group (USA) Inc.
The "J" design is a trademark of Penguin Group (USA) Inc.

For information, address: The Berkley Publishing Group,
a division of Penguin Group (USA) Inc.,
375 Hudson Street, New York, New York 10014.

ISBN: 978-0-515-15317-0

PUBLISHING HISTORY
Jove mass-market edition / April 2013

PRINTED IN THE UNITED STATES OF AMERICA

10 9 8 7 6 5 4 3 2 1

Cover illustration by Sergio Giovine.

ONE

In 1853, a local Shasta County newspaper reported there wasn't a river, creek, gulch, or ravine in Shasta County that didn't contain gold. Since that time, gold was being taken out of Mad Mule Valley in seemingly unending proportions . . .

Ed O'Neil finished writing the letter, reread the two pages, and nodded. Satisfied that the letter said what he wanted it to say, he folded it and put it in an envelope. He sealed it, and then addressed it. At that moment the door opened and Danny Lyons came in, stamping his feet to get some of the mud off them.

"You wanted to see me, boss?"

"That's right," O'Neil said. "I got a job for you, Danny."

"Whatever you want, boss," Danny said. "You know that."

"I want you to deliver this personally."

Lyons walked up to his boss's desk and took the letter from him. He read the name on the envelope and his eyes widened. Then he read the address.

"Personal, boss."

"That's right."

"B-But . . . you could mail it."

"It would take too long."

"Naw, they're real good these days—"

"I don't trust them," O'Neil said. "I trust you, Danny."

"What about a telegram?"

"Not enough room."

"But . . . I'd have to ride for days . . ."

"I've arranged for you to ride in shifts," O'Neil said. "Horses will be waiting for you at certain stations along the way."

"You mean . . . like the Pony Express?"

"Just like the Pony Express."

"Boss . . . some of those guys died."

"You won't die."

Lyons, who was twenty-eight, said, "Boss, them riders, they was kids. I ain't no kid."

"You're young enough," O'Neil said. "And I'm payin' you this."

He handed Lyons another envelope. This time the younger man looked inside. His eyes widened again, and his eyebrows shot up.

"All of this?"

"Yeah."

"You're givin' this to me now?"

"I am."

"But . . . what if I just leave and keep goin', and never deliver the letter?"

"You won't," O'Neil said. "I trust you, son."

"I don't know what to say," Lyons answered.

"Just say you'll do it."

"This'll take days."

"I know it will," Ed O'Neil said. "After you're done, you can take the train back—that is, if you want to come back."

Lyons put the two envelopes together in his hands.

"I'll come back, boss," he said. "You need me."

"You're right, son," O'Neil said. "I do." He stopped, and

put his hand out. Lyons stepped forward and shook the older man's hand.

"I'll get it done, boss," Danny Lyons said. "I promise."

"I know you will, Danny," Ed O'Neil said. "I know you will."

LABYRINTH, TEXAS

"You know what your problem is?" Rick Hartman asked Clint Adams.

"What's my problem?"

"You've done everything," Rick said. "You've been all over the country, you've been out of the country, you've owned saloons and gambling halls, gold mines, hell, you've even run for political office. Jesus, what's left?"

"*That's* my problem, then," Clint said.

"What?"

"I need to decide what to do next," Clint said. "What haven't I done yet?"

"Well," Rick said, giving it some thought, "you haven't been to China or Japan."

"I don't want to go to China or Japan," Clint said.

"Why not?"

"Too far," Clint said. "It would take too long."

"I guess you're right."

They were sitting at a table in Rick's Place, the saloon/gambling palace owned by Rick in Labyrinth, Texas. Clint had been in Labyrinth a week, and was itching to move on. But to go where, and do what? Those were the questions.

He and Rick were discussing it over a few mugs of beer. Around them, Rick's Place was doing its usual brisk business. The tables were busy, and the girls were, too, carrying drinks to gamblers, spectators, and men who were there just to drink.

"How do you do it?" Clint asked Rick.

"How do I do what?"

"You never leave here," Clint said. "You never leave Labyrinth."

"I have, too."

"What, twice in the last ten years?"

"That means I've left."

"Okay," Clint said, "then how do you leave only once every five years? I'd go crazy."

"That's because you don't own anything."

"I do, too," Clint said. "I've got pieces of saloons, and mines, as you pointed out—"

"Around the country, yeah," Rick said, "but no place you call home. Not really."

"Home," Clint said, staring at his half-empty mug.

"This place is my home," Rick said. "I love it. I don't want to leave."

"I guess I can't blame you for that," Clint said. He lifted his mug and finished the contents. "It's just a little late in life for me to try putting down roots."

"And I can understand that," Rick said. "But you know, there is something you haven't done yet."

"What's that?"

"You haven't gotten married."

Clint stared at his friend, then said, "I think I need a shot of whiskey after that."

Rick raised his hand to attract the attention of one of the girls.

TWO

Clint rolled over in bed and looked at the girl lying next to him. The sun coming in through the hotel window turned her skin to gold. She was lying naked on her belly, her small breasts crushed beneath her. She was blond, so there was a fine downy growth of blond hairs on her that picked up the sun, hence the glow.

She was a slender girl with a fine bottom, long legs, and smooth, pale skin. He reached out to touch her buttocks, enjoying the feel as he rubbed his hand over them.

She moaned, moved her bottom a bit, then rolled to her left to peer up at him. He saw one teacup-sized, pink-nippled breast.

"Are you tryin' to wake me up?" she asked.

"I am."

"But you wore me out last night."

"And I'm looking forward to wearing you out this morning, too, Hannah."

She rolled onto her back and giggled.

"I'm kinda lookin' forward to that, too."

He moved over her, kissed her, reached down to touch her between the legs, rubbing her gently with his fingertips until she was nice and wet and squirming. He pressed the head of his fully erect cock to her wet slit and pushed it in. She gasped, her long legs coming up and wrapping around him.

"Come on, Gunsmith," Hannah said into his ear in a husky whisper, "ride me."

He proceeded to do just that . . .

The rider came into town at a gallop, the gray beneath him shiny with sweat. He slowed to locate the livery, then dismounted in front.

"Jesus, mister," the liveryman said, coming out with a broken bridle in his hands, "you tryin' ta kill yerself or the horse?"

Gasping, the rider said, "The Gunsmith. I'm lookin' for Clint Adams. Is he in town?"

"He sure is," the man said. "His horse is still right here."

"I gotta find 'im," the man said. "Where is he?"

The liveryman knew he could get into trouble giving out the name of Clint Adams's hotel, so he said, "Yer best bet is to go over to Rick's Place. He's usually there."

"Th-Thanks."

The rider turned to leave, but at that moment one of his legs gave out. He stumbled, almost fell, then righted himself.

"You okay, son?" the liveryman asked.

"I been ridin' kinda hard . . . for days . . . tryin' ta get here," the rider said.

"You mean . . . like the Pony Express?"

"Yeah," Danny Lyons said, "exactly like the Pony Express."

When Lyons got to Rick's Place, he found the front door locked. That's when he realized how early it was. But he'd risked his neck riding in the dark, so a locked door wasn't about to stop him.

He started pounding his fist on it.

Inside, Rick Hartman was just sitting down to his breakfast when the pounding started on the door.

"See who that is," he told the bartender, "and tell them to go away and come back when we're open."

"Sure, boss," the bartender said.

Rick started on his eggs while the bartender handled the door.

"I don't care if yer closed," a voice shouted, "I gotta deliver this letter to the Gunsmith."

Rick looked up as a young man pushed past the bartender and entered the saloon. He looked as if he was ready to pack it in after a long ride.

"What the hell—" Rick said.

"Sorry, boss," the bartender said. "I'll get 'im out of here."

"Where's the Gunsmith?" the man demanded.

"What makes you think the Gunsmith is here?" Rick asked.

"The man at the livery stable told me," the man said. "Look, I been ridin' a long time . . ." At that moment his eyes rolled up and he started to fall. The bartender caught him, and Rick sprang from his chair to help.

"Sit him over here," Rick said, and they took the man to his table. "Get me another cup."

"Yeah, boss."

The man came to almost immediately and asked, "What happened?"

"You fainted. When's the last time you ate?"

"I ain't . . . ate in a long while."

"Well, here," Rick said. He reached for his plate of bacon and eggs and slid it across the table to the man. He handed him a fork. "Start eatin'."

"I gotta find Clint Adams—"

"You'll find him," Rick said. "Eat, and have some coffee."

The man put a piece of bacon into his mouth, then grabbed

the fork and started stuffing his mouth with eggs. The barman came with another cup, and Rick filled it with coffee. The weary man grabbed it and drank it down, unmindful of how hot it was.

"Take it easy," Rick said as the man started to cough.

The man wiped his mouth on his sleeve and then looked at Rick.

"Mister, it's real important I deliver this letter to Clint Adams. Is he here?"

"He's not," Rick said, "but he will be by the time you finish eating. I guarantee it."

That seemed to satisfy the man, and he went back to his eating.

THREE

Clint was down between Hannah Davis's smooth thighs, licking and sucking up as much of her nectar as he could, when there was a knock on the door.

"Go away!" he shouted.

"Oh, God," Hannah said, squirming beneath him, "don't stop."

The knocking didn't stop either.

"Damn it!" Clint shouted.

"Rick sent me, Mr. Adams," a voice said. "He says it's important."

Clint looked up at Hannah, whose beautiful eyes were closed as she bit her bottom lip.

"Don't go away," he told her.

"What?" she asked, opening her eyes. "What are you doin'?"

"Answering the door. Somebody's banging on it," he said, pulling on his pants. "It will only take a minute."

"It better!" she said, eyes flashing. "You're not done here."

He opened the door, didn't know the man standing there, but did recognize him as someone Rick used to run errands.

"What is it?"

The young man looked past him at the naked girl on the bed.

"Oh, I'm sorry—"

"Just tell me what's going on," Clint said.

"A man rode into town, says he's got a letter for you."

"A letter? That can't wait?"

"Rick says to tell you the man rode Pony Express style, for days, to get this letter to you."

"Who's the letter from?"

"I dunno. I don't think Rick even knows," the young man said.

"Where's the man who delivered it?"

"He's at Rick's. They're waitin' for you."

"Okay," Clint said, "okay, tell them I'll be right there."

"Yessir."

Clint closed the door, turned, and looked at Hannah, who was staring at him.

"Right there?" she asked.

"Well," he said, undoing his pants, "not *right* there . . ."

Twenty minutes later Clint walked into Rick's Place. His friend was seated at a table with another man, who looked completely done in.

"Well, here he is," Rick said.

"Sorry," Clint said. "I had to . . . finish."

"Uh-huh," Rick said. "This fella's name is Danny, and he has a letter for you."

The done-in man looked up at Clint and asked, "Are you Clint Adams?"

"I am," Clint said. "Who're you?"

"Danny Lyons," the young man said. He held out an envelope. "This is for you."

Clint accepted the letter, thought about asking who it was from, then decided to just open it to find out.

The room was quiet as he read it. Only Rick, Danny Lyons, and the bartender were present, and it was as if they were holding their breath.

"So what is it?" Rick asked.

"It's two pages, Rick," Clint said, "from a friend of mine in Shasta County."

"California?"

"Yep. Ed O'Neil."

"I heard you talk about him."

"Yeah," Clint said. "Look, his handwriting's not easy to read. Can you get Danny here a room and a bed so he can get some rest? I'm going to sit and try to decipher this thing."

"Yeah, sure," Rick said. He waved at the bartender. "I'll have Harve take him over to the hotel."

"I'll foot the bill," Clint said.

"Suits me," Rick said.

They both looked at Danny Lyons, who was either asleep, or had passed out again.

"Okay," Rick said, standing up, "I better help Harve with this guy."

"I'll be right here," Clint said.

"Have some coffee while you're readin'," Rick said. "I'll be right back."

Harve got Clint a cup before he and Rick left. Clint poured himself some coffee and sipped while he read.

FOUR

Clint got to the dock early, before the ship had even arrived. There were others eagerly awaiting the arrival of their loved ones. Clint, on the other hand, was waiting for two women he'd never met, had never even seen. But he'd made a promise to meet them.

The two-page letter had laid out, in a handwriting that resembled ink on a chicken's feet, exactly what Ed O'Neil wanted Clint to do. And when Rick Hartman got back from sticking Danny in a hotel, he'd told him the story . . .

"It seems," Clint had explained, "that Ed has arranged for a woman to come over from Ireland, to marry him."

"A mail-order bride?" Rick asked.

"Yeah, I guess that's it, only this one's bringing somebody with her. An older sister."

"Wait," Rick said, "isn't O'Neil . . ."

"Yep," Clint said, "over sixty."

"And he's gonna marry the younger sister?"

"That's the way it looks."

"So how old are these women?"

"He doesn't say," Clint said. "Just that they're arriving

in New York next week, and he wants me to meet them there, and escort them cross-country to him."

"Why you?" Rick asked. "Why doesn't he just hire somebody to escort them? This isn't the kind of thing you do."

"He's asking me to do it as a favor, Rick."

Rick rolled his eyes.

"Well, we know you do those, don't we?"

"I owe him," Clint said.

Rick held up his hand. "You don't have to explain," he said. "When are you leavin'?"

"Tomorrow," Clint said. "I want to get to New York in plenty of time."

"New York."

"It's been a while since I was there," Clint said.

"I guess that's as good a reason as any to go," Rick said. "Does this guy O'Neil do what I think he does in Shasta?"

"Yes," Clint said. "He's got a gold mine. A pretty good strike."

"Is he payin' you for this little trip?"

"No," Clint said. "I said it was a favor."

"So you did. Well, I've got to wish you luck seein' two ladies across the country by . . . what? Covered wagon?"

"It's as good a way as any . . ."

Clint watched as the huge ship arrived, barely missing the dock as it did. Whoever was piloting the big boat had a light touch.

It took a while but eventually they lowered two planks, one for passengers, and one to offload cargo. People crowded the dock as passengers began to offload. Clint watched as sweethearts, husbands, wives, and families were reunited. There were also passengers who were met by no one, who simply went their own way.

And then there were two ladies.

Since Clint knew that O'Neil was fat—the last time he saw him—and sixty, he expected the prospective bride to be sixty—and her older sister even older. These two girls were young, probably in their twenties and only a few years apart. He wouldn't have even considered them except for two things—they were standing there with their bags at their feet, looking around, and they had red hair—Irish red hair.

Clint approached them. As he came closer, one of them noticed him and nudged the other. O'Neil's letter had given him their names. Bridget and Bride Shaughnessy.

"Miss Shaughnessy?" he asked.

"Yes," one of them said, "we are Bridget and Bride Shaughnessy. And who might you be?"

She spoke with a lovely Irish lilt that gave him pause for a moment. The other girl—Bride, he assumed, pronounced "Bridey"—stared at him. He couldn't believe that she was to be O'Neil's "bride." She looked all of twenty.

"My name is Clint Adams," Clint said. "Ed O'Neil sent me to pick you up."

"And how are we to know you are who you say you are, an emissary from Mr. O'Neil?" the one who was probably Bridget asked.

"I have a letter he sent me," Clint said. "Would you recognize his handwriting? His signature?"

"His handwriting is like chicken scratches," she said, "and his signature is his mark."

Clint nodded, stepped forward, and handed her O'Neil's letter. She opened it, briefly scanned it, and then handed it back.

"It looks like his writing," she said. "Greetings, Mr. Adams. How are you related to Mr. O'Neil?"

"We're friends, ma'am."

"Well," she said, "we told Mr. O'Neil that we wanted to see your beautiful country before my sister would marry him. Are you able to arrange that?"

"I am, ma'am."

"Well, this is Bride," she said, "she is to marry Mr. O'Neil. I am her older sister, Bridget."

"If you don't mind, ma'am," Clint asked, "just how old are you?"

"I am twenty-four," she said, "and Bride is twenty-two. I do not know about your country, Mr. Adams, but in our country we are considered old maids. I hope you will not hold that against us."

Clint looked at the two beautiful Irish girls and said, "Not me, ma'am. Are these all your bags?"

"They are," she said. "We left most of our belongings behind and took only what we could carry."

"Just wait here, ladies," he said, "and I'll get somebody to help us carry them."

Hidden among the crowd on the docks, two men watched as Clint met the two women.

"You see what I see?" one of them asked.

"Yeah," the second said.

"We're gonna have to find out who he is."

"How we gonna do that?"

"We're gonna follow them," the first man said. "See where they go. Keep our ears open. We'll find out who this man is." His name was Jack Ahern, and his partner was Phil Kemper.

"Maybe we should just grab the women," Kemper said. "Look, he's goin' to find somebody to carry the bags. We can take them now."

"Not without findin' out who he is first," Ahern said. "We've gotta be careful. We mess this up, we don't get paid."

"Yeah, okay," Kemper said. After all, getting paid was the most important part.

FIVE

Clint got two stevedores to carry the Shaughnessy sisters' bags to the street, where he had a cab waiting. They loaded the half a dozen bags and one trunk onto the wagon, tied them down, and then helped the ladies get in.

"Will we be going to a hotel?" Bridget asked. "My sister and I are very tired."

"I'm sorry, Bridget," he said, "but we're headed for the railroad station."

"Railroad?" she asked. "Are we not to see New York City?"

"As much of it as you can see between here and the station," he said. "We're taking a train out this afternoon."

"Train?" Bride asked. "I thought we were to see your country on horseback?"

"Nobody said anything about horseback, ma'am," Clint said. "We'll be taking the train as far as Saint Louis. From there we'll travel the rest of the way by wagon. That's the part of the country you want to see."

The two sisters exchanged a glance, and then Bridget said, "Very well, Mr. Adams. We are in your hands."

"Thank you, Miss Shaughnessy." He leaned forward and tapped the driver on the shoulder. "Train station."

"Right!"

At Penn Station they loaded the luggage onto the train, except for one bag each that the girls wanted to keep with them. Clint had one carpetbag that he also kept. The ladies were shown to the compartment Clint had obtained for them, and then he was shown to the one right next to it. There was a connecting door that he had no intention of using. The money for the compartments, and tickets, would be reimbursed to him when they all arrived in Shasta County.

"You can rest for a few hours," Clint told them, "and then I'll come and get you so we can all go to the dining car."

"That will be fine, Mr. Adams," Bridget said.

He touched the brim of his hat and said, "Ladies," then went to his own compartment.

On the platform the two men looked at each other.

"Now what do we do?" Kemper asked.

"What we were hired to do," Ahern said. "If that means we gotta take a rail trip, then we gotta do it. Come on, let's get some tickets."

Kemper grabbed his friend's arm.

"What happens if he sees us?" he asked.

"That'll be his problem," Ahern said. "If he forces our hand, we kill him."

That satisfied Kemper. They went to a ticket window.

When Clint Adams was gone, Bride said, "Bridget," and pointed to the connecting door.

"Don't worry," her sister told her. She went to the door and tried it. "It's firmly locked."

"But from which side?" Bride asked.

Bridget opened her bag and took out an ancient-looking .25 caliber Webley Irish pistol.

"We are armed," she told her sister confidently.

"I'm still afraid," Bride said, sitting on her berth.

Bridget went and sat beside her sister, took her hand.

"Afraid of what?"

"Everything," Bride said. "This country, that man . . . Mr. O'Neil."

"You haven't even met Mr. O'Neil," Bridget said.

"I know it," Bride said, "and yet you expect me to marry him."

"The man has a gold mine, Bride," Bridget said. "Keep your mind on that."

"I am," the younger sister said. "That is what keeps me going."

Bridget squeezed her sister's hand.

"Just do as I say," she told her, "and we'll be fine."

"A-All right."

"Now get some rest." Bridget stood up, so that her sister could recline on her berth. The upper berth had been opened by the porter, but Bridget did not climb up. She set about changing her clothes, removed her dress, and took another, simpler frock from her bag. The valley between her pert breasts was heavily freckled. She held the dress to her and thought a moment.

"He's very good looking," she said.

"Who?" Bride asked.

"Mr. Adams. Don't you think?"

"He scares me," Bride said again.

"Me, you."

"But you said you weren't scared."

"Oh, I don't mean he frightens me," Bridget said, "he was . . . scares me a little. Here." She touched her belly.

"Bridget," Bride said warningly, sitting up. "No."

"What do you mean, no?"

"You said you wouldn't do that," Bride said. "You promised you'd control yourself."

"Oh, I know I did," she said, "but he's very . . . masculine, isn't he?"

"Oh God," Bride said. She lay back down and put her hand to her forehead.

SIX

Clint went to his compartment and sat looking out the window. People were still rushing by, trying to make their trains on time. The two ladies were safely installed in their own accommodations. That part of the job was over.

He was surprised at the youth of the two women, especially considering the age of Ed O'Neil. He wondered if O'Neil knew he'd be marrying a girl forty years his junior.

It was true, women who made it out of their teens without being married used to be considered old maids, but wasn't the country—the world—a more progressive place than that? Clint had met many women over the years—in their twenties and even thirties—who were still single. Not one of them acted like an old maid. But these two were from Ireland. Things must have been different there.

He sat back, thought about taking off his boots for a couple of hours. His gun and holster were wrapped up in his pack. He had his Colt New Line stuck in his belt. As soon as they got far enough away from New York, he'd take the holster out and put it on. Then he'd feel much more comfortable.

He closed his eyes as the train jerked to a start, dozing very lightly while the train moved out of the station and began its journey . . .

                          *   *   *

Ahern and Kemper got seats in a passenger car.

"We gotta find out where they are," Ahern said. "But we can't let the cowboy see us."

"Look," Kemper said, "we're from the city, and he's from the country. If we were on his trail, maybe he'd spot us, but this is our turf."

"You got that right," Ahern said, "but we'll have to act separately. You take a walk, see what you can find out. I'll wait here."

"I'm hungry."

"We'll get somethin' to eat when you get back."

Kemper nodded and left his seat.

After a couple of hours Clint stood up, cleaned himself up a bit, and put on some fresh clothes. Considering himself decent enough to be in the company of two lovely Irish lasses, he left his compartment to escort them to the dining car.

Bridget finished tying the knot at the back of Bride's dress when there was a knock on the door.

"Who could that be?" Bride asked.

"Relax," Bridget said. "It can only be Mr. Adams."

Bride's dress covered her from head to toe, but Bridget's showed a good portion of her freckled chest.

"Aren't you going to cover up?" Bride asked.

"Relax, dear sister," Bridget said. "Everything will be fine."

She went to answer the door.

As the door opened, Clint's eye fell right where Bridget wanted it to fall, on her chest.

"Mr. Adams," she said, giving him a smile. "Right on time."

"Am I?"

"Yes, indeed," she said. "We are very hungry."

He looked past her at her sister, who appeared more frightened than tired.

"I'm here to take you to the dining car," Clint said.

"Indeed," Bridget said. "Are you coming, Bride?"

"Yes," her sister said.

In the hall outside, there was no room for them to walk abreast, so rather than give each girl one of his arms, Clint indicated that they should walk ahead of him. He followed them to the dining car, where they were seated at a table.

Outside the window, the city had fallen away and countryside was whizzing by.

"We're going very fast," Bride said.

"Yes, we are," Clint said, "but don't worry, it's very safe."

A white-coated, white-gloved, bow-tied black waiter came over and asked, "Somethin' fo' the ladies and the gentleman?"

"Do you have steak?" Bridget asked.

"Yes, ma'am," the man said, "we's got mighty good steaks."

"Oh, Bridget," Bride said, "steak."

"And potatoes," the man said.

"Oh," Bride said, "no potatoes, please."

"But lots of other vegetables," Bridget said. "Onions? Carrots?"

"And peas?" the waiter asked.

"Oh yes, please," Bride said. "Sweet peas."

"And you, suh?"

"A steak," Clint said, "and I'll take all the potatoes the ladies aren't having."

"Yes, suh."

"And all the rest."

"Suh," the waiter said, "and to drink?"

"Tea," Bride said.

"Tea," Bridget said.

"Coffee," Clint said.

"Comin' up, folks," the waiter said.

"So," Clint asked, "are you both relaxed?"

It was obvious that Bride was going to leave most of the talking to Bridget, who said, "Yes, we're fine. It was an arduous trip on the ship and, at times, quite frightening."

"Were you . . . accosted at all on the ship?" he asked.

"No, no," she said, "the crew stayed away from us for the most part. It was frightening once or twice, but we came through it quite unscathed, thanks be to the Lord."

The waiter returned with their tea and coffee. The ladies added sugar and stirred it in for a long time. The waiter had also brought lemons, which they used. Clint simply drank his coffee black with nothing in it.

Bride sipped her tea and said to Bridget, "Oh, this is heavenly."

"Wait until you have the steak," Clint said.

"It's been so long since we've had beef," Bridget said. "I mean, good beef."

"I suppose there were hardships for you in your country?" Clint asked.

"Yes," Bridget said, "we were living under great hardship when . . . well, when Mr. O'Neil came to our rescue."

"And how did that occur, if I may ask?" Clint said.

The girls exchanged a look, and then Bridget said, "He did not tell you?"

"I know only what was in the letter," Clint said. "I haven't seen Ed in some time."

"And yet he asked you to do this?"

"We're friends," Clint said. "It doesn't matter how long it's been since we've seen each other. We're still friends."

"That is very admirable," Bridget said. "Perhaps he should explain the whole thing to you when he sees you again."

"Perhaps you're right," Clint said. "I didn't mean to be intrusive."

"You are very well spoken for a Westerner, Mr. Adams," Bridget said. He didn't want to insult her, but she was better spoken than most Irish he'd met.

"I was born in the East," he said.

"I see."

The waiter came then with their plates, and they suspended their conversation while he laid them out. Bride's eyes went wide with glee at the sight of the steaming steak and onions, as well as all the other vegetables.

When the waiter withdrew, Clint said, "Well, I guess we'd better eat."

The girls didn't have to be told twice.

Kemper returned to the passenger car, sat next to Ahern.

"You see them?"

"They're in the dining car."

"All right," Ahern said, "we'll have to wait until they finish eating, then we can get something."

"We gonna find out where they're sleepin'?"

"We are," Ahern said, "but we can do that by slipping a dollar to a conductor, or porter. Just relax, Kemper. Just relax."

SEVEN

The steak wasn't particularly good, but it was what Clint expected from railroad food. On the other hand, the Shaughnessy sisters loved their meal, consumed it with great gusto. The waiter brought them more tea to wash it all down.

When they were finished and he had cleared the plates, the waiter asked, "Would the ladies like dessert?"

"Dessert?" Bride asked.

"We have several kinds of pie—" the waiter started.

"May we have one of each?" Bride asked. She looked at Bridget, Clint, and the waiter, not at all sure who would make that decision.

"I don't see why not," Clint said.

"Very well, suh," the waiter said. "One slice of each pie."

Bride slapped her hands together happily and Bridget smiled her thanks at Clint.

"Thank you so much," he said. "She loves sweets."

"Then she should have as much as she can take," Clint said. "What about you?"

She looked him in the eye and said, "My pleasures run to other things."

For a moment he wondered if she was trying to send him a message, but he didn't know her well enough to judge.

The waiter came with slices of apple, cherry, peach, and rhubarb pie. The girls gave the pie all their attention. Clint managed a small piece of rhubarb and a larger piece of peach, but other than that, the girls ate it all.

When they were done, they sat and watched the country-side go by outside the window. Clint ordered more coffee, decided not to ask the girls any more questions for the time being.

Instead, the girls began to ask him questions about the United States, which he answered as best he could. They also wanted to know about what they called "the Wild West." During that conversation, realization dawned on Bridget, and Clint saw it on her face.

"But wait . . ." she said.

"Yes?"

"You said your name is Clint Adams?"

"That's right."

"What is it, sister?" Bride asked.

Bridget looked back at her sister and said, "Clint Adams, Bride. We have heard stories of him."

Then, suddenly, it also dawned on Bride.

"You mean . . . the Gunsmith?"

Both girls turned their heads and looked at Clint in awe.

"I hope this won't change our relationship in any way," he said to them.

It was difficult for the girls to talk to him after that, so he paid the bill for the food and escorted them back to their compartment.

"Get a good night's rest," he said. "I'll see you in the morning."

They both nodded. He closed the door and went to his own compartment. This time when he got inside, he removed his boots and rubbed his feet. He stared out his own window for a time, and then somebody knocked on his door.

When he slid the door open, Bridget stood there.

"May I come in?"

"If it's all right with you, it's all right with me," he said. "I can leave the door open."

"I believe I can trust you," she said. "After all, you are a legend."

"Come in."

She entered and he closed the door. He waved her to the seat he had just vacated, by the window. He sat on his berth.

"My sister and I are sorry we did not recognize you immediately," she said. "We are sorry we questioned you."

"It makes sense to be careful," he said. "That's all you were doing."

"We're honored that Mr. O'Neil sent such an important man to escort us to him."

"Like I said," he replied, "Ed and I are friends."

"Then I am more impressed with him than I already was."

"Tell me," Clint said, "how did Ed and your sister first meet?"

"Through the mail. Mr. O'Neil still has family in Ireland. When it became known he was looking for a wife, Bridget and I stepped forward. We both exchanged letters with him. He chose her."

"Is that all right with you?" Clint asked. "That he chose your sister over you?"

"It didn't matter which one of us he chose," she said. "We knew we would both come to this country."

"So you're happy the way it worked out?" Clint asked.

"Let us say we are satisfied."

"Well," Clint said, "if you're satisfied, so am I."

She nodded, and stood. She stared at him for a moment, wet her lips. He looked at her freckled skin, saw that her chest was heaving. She was breathing heavily.

"Are you all right?" he asked.

"I am . . . fine," she said. "I just wanted to apologize to you."

"And you have," Clint said. "Now why don't you go and get some rest."

"Yes."

"We have a few more days of rail travel—we'll switch trains once—before we get to the point where we will switch to wagon travel."

"Is it still possible to go on horseback? My sister and I are good riders."

"We can discuss that when the time comes," Clint told her.

"Very well. Good night, then."

He opened the door for her, watched her walk to her own room and enter. For a moment he thought she might try to seduce him, but maybe she didn't know how.

Or maybe she just wasn't ready.

EIGHT

It was several days later when they disembarked in Saint Louis and Clint installed them all in the Magnolia Hotel. He had left his horse, Eclipse, there in the capable hands of a smithy he knew would take good care of him.

When he put the ladies in their room, Bridget asked, "Will we be able to see anything of the city?"

"Yes," Clint said, "I'll take you out for supper, but first I have to go and check on my horse."

"And horses for us?"

"A wagon anyway," Clint said. "We'll need a wagon in order to transport your luggage."

"That makes sense," she said.

"I'll be back in a little while. Get some rest."

"It seems like you are always telling us that," Bridget said. "Hurry back, please."

"I will."

He left them at the Magnolia and went over to his friend's blacksmith shop.

Ahern and Kemper followed Clint and the two women to the Magnolia Hotel.

"You ever been in Saint Louis before?" Kemper asked.

"Yeah," Ahern said. "There's a smaller hotel around the corner we can get a room at."

"Then what?"

"They gotta be stayin' overnight," Ahern said. "I'm gonna send a telegram and get some instructions, but I think this is where we're gonna make our move. Come on."

As Clint entered the shop, Jerry Trask looked up from the horse he was shoeing and spotted him.

"There ya are," he said. "I was hopin' you wouldn't come back and I could keep Eclipse for myself."

"At least that way I'd know he was in good hands."

The two men shook hands.

"How's he doing?" Clint asked.

"He's fine," Trask said. "He's been eatin' well, has a nice shine to his coat."

"Good."

"Just a little depressed," Trask added. "I think the big guy missed you."

"That's good to hear," Clint said. "I missed him, too."

"He's in the back. Lemme finish this horse here, and then we'll talk and have a drink."

"Okay."

Trask went back to the horse he was shoeing while Clint walked to Eclipse's stall.

"Hey, big fella," he said laying his hands first on the horse's rump, then his neck. Eclipse reacted to the familiar touch. "How you doin', boy?"

The big Arabian nuzzled his hand and Clint rubbed his neck hard.

"We'll be out on the trail soon, big fella," Clint said. "You been cooped up long enough."

"Clint!"

Clint left the stall, found Trask standing there.

"Come on, I got a bottle in my office. Let's have a drink before you leave."

"I won't be taking him out 'til morning, Jerry," Clint said, "but a drink sounds good."

They went into Trask's office.

"You like him," Bride said.

"Who?" Bridget asked.

"Mr. Adams." Bridget was braiding Bride's hair, and looked at her sister in the mirror.

"You know I do."

"Did you . . . on the train, did you . . . do anything?" Bride asked.

"No," Bridget said. "I wanted to. I almost did. But I promised you, didn't I?"

"Yes, you did."

"Well," Bridget said, "I may not always, but this time I am keeping my promise."

For now, she thought.

Ahern came into the room, and Kemper looked up from the bed he was reclining on.

"Did you get an answer?"

"I did."

"So what do we do?"

Ahern sat on his own bed.

"We take 'em now," he said. "Those are our orders. They get no farther than this."

"So when do we do it?"

"After," Ahern said.

"After what?"

"After I get to the Magnolia and find out once and for all who we're dealin' with."

NINE

Clint knocked on the door, which was opened by Bridget.

"Thank God you're back," she said.

"Why? Is something wrong?"

"We're hungry," she said.

"Oh," he said, "well, we can take care of that right away. Are you ready to go?"

"We are ready."

They left the room and walked down to the hotel lobby with him.

Outside Clint said, "We'll walk. There's a restaurant not very far from here."

There was still plenty of daylight, so the girls were able to see something of the city. And its buildings.

"Some of them are so big," Bride remarked to her sister. "I have never seen such big buildings like these, and the ones we saw in New York."

"You won't see big buildings like these when we get further West," Clint told them, "but you'll see some very big country."

"We have some big country in Ireland, Mr. Adams," Bridget said. "Big and green."

"I'm sure you have, Miss Shaughnessy."

"Have you never been?" she asked.

"I never have," he said. "England is as close as I came. And I think for the remainder of the trip you and your sister should start calling me Clint."

"Very well, Clint," she said, "and you may call us by our Christian names—Bridget and Bride."

"That's great," he said. "Here we are."

They stopped in front of a restaurant with a huge front window covered in stenciled lettering.

"Steak?" Bride asked.

"Steak," Clint said, "and as much as you want."

They went inside.

Ahern and Kemper entered the Magnolia Hotel lobby and stopped just inside.

"Stay here and keep watch," Ahern said. "Let me know if you see them."

"How?"

"Figure it out," Ahern said. He walked to the front desk.

"Can I help you, sir?"

"Yeah, I'm lookin' for a friend of mine, supposed to be registered here."

"And his name?"

"Jones," Ahern said, "Roger Jones."

The clerk looked at the register very intently, then said, "I'm sorry, sir, we don't seem to have your friend registered here."

"Really?" Ahern asked. "That's odd, because a friend of mine said he saw him here yesterday."

"And he registered with us?"

"That's what I was told," Ahern said. "Oh wait, I was also told he had two women with him—two Irish women. Young and pretty, they are. Maybe he registered them, but went someplace else himself."

"I suppose that could be," the clerk said. "I would hate

to think—well, we did have two young ladies register with us yesterday. Their name is Shaughnessy."

"That's it, that's the name," Ahern said. "I was tryin' to remember their last name. Are you sure Jones didn't register?"

"Well . . . there was a gentleman with them, and he did register, but his name is not Jones."

"Are you sure?"

"Yes, sir, quite sure. You see, I remember, because . . . well . . ." He leaned on the desk and lowered his voice. "The man was Clint Adams."

"Clint Adams?"

"The Gunsmith," the clerk said.

"Well, of course," Ahern said, reacting quickly, "I knew it was Clint Adams, but I thought he was going to register under the name *Jones*, not under his real name."

"Ah, I see," the clerk said, straightening up.

"Are they in their rooms now, do you know?" Ahern asked.

"Oh, no, sir," the clerk said. "I saw them go out just a few minutes ago . . . to dinner, I believe."

"I see," Ahern said. "Well, thanks. I'll stop by later."

"Very well, sir."

"Oh, one more thing."

"Yes, sir?"

"Don't bother mentioning to my old buddy Clint that I was lookin' for him. I want to surprise him."

"As you wish, sir."

Ahern slipped the man a dollar and said, "Thanks."

He walked over to the door, where Kemper was waiting, fidgeting from one foot to the other.

"Well, what—" Kemper started.

"Outside," Ahern said. "Let's get out of here!"

TEN

Bridget and Bride both ordered steak, and once again Clint ended up with a plate almost filled with extra potatoes.

"This is marvelous," Bridget said.

"So much better than the steak we had on the train," Bride said.

"The steaks will get better the further West we get," Clint told them.

"Really?" Bride asked. The only time she had spoken directly to him at all the entire trip was about steak.

"Oh yes," Clint said. "If there's one thing we know how to do in the West, it's cook steak."

"I heard you were also very good at riding and roping," Bridget said.

"Oh yeah, that, too," Clint said.

"And bronco riding," Bridget said. "Can you ride a bronco, Clint?"

"I have in the past," Clint said.

Bride swallowed the piece of steak she'd been chewing and asked, "What's a bronco?"

"The Gunsmith?" Kemper asked as they walked back to their own hotel. "The goddamned Gunsmith?"

"That's what he said."

"Maybe he's wrong," Kemper said. "Or maybe he's lyin'."

"He was tellin' the truth," Ahern said. "It's the Gunsmith."

"Well, I didn't sign on to face the Gunsmith," Kemper said. "We need to get out of this."

"Not what I was thinkin'," Ahern said.

"You mean you want to face him?"

"I mean," Ahern said, "if we're goin' up against the Gunsmith, I want more money."

"Ah!"

"And I mean a lot more money," Ahern said.

"But we can't spend the money if we're dead."

"Don't worry," Ahern said. "I've got a plan."

"A plan to stay alive?"

"Yes."

"And still make money?"

"Yes."

"Well, then," Kemper said, "I'm listening."

This time at dessert they settled on one piece of pie each—peach for Clint, cherry for Bridget, and apple for Bride.

"What can we do after this?" Bridget asked.

"Well, we can walk around and look at the city a bit more," Clint said, "but we should get back to the hotel before dark."

"Let me guess, Clint," Bridget said, "you want us to rest some more."

"Yes," he said, "we're going to get an early start tomorrow."

"Did you get us a wagon already?"

"I made arrangements with a friend of mine," Clint said. "The wagon, team, and my horse will be waiting for us in front of our hotel in the morning."

"Shouldn't Bride and I shop for some new clothes?" Bridget asked.

"We'll do that in Council Bluffs," Clint said, "but there probably are some clothes you should put in one trunk."

"Which trunk?" she asked.

"One you won't be opening again for a long time."

ELEVEN

Clint walked the ladies around the city a bit more, and then they went back to the hotel.

"What a beautiful city," Bride said. She seemed to finally be loosening up a bit, although the comment was directed to her sister.

"Yes, it is," she said. "And a beautiful river."

"I would love to ride a riverboat," Bride said.

"Can we?" Bridget asked Clint.

"I'm afraid not," Clint said. "But once your sister marries Ed, I'm sure he'd be happy to take you ladies on the river-boat."

"Mr. O'Neil is a hard worker," Bridget observed.

"Yes, he is," Clint said.

As they walked past the front desk, Clint noticed the clerk looking at him with a worried expression. When the clerk noticed Clint looking, he averted his eyes.

"Why don't you girls go on up to your room," Clint said. "I'll be along later to answer any questions and say good night."

"Very well," Bridget said. "Come along, Bride."

He watched as they walked up the stairs, then turned and went over to the front desk.

"Mr. Adams," the clerk said nervously. "W-What can I do for you, sir?"

"You can tell me why you're so nervous," Clint said.

"Nervous? I'm not nervous."

"Come on, son," Clint said. "Don't make me drag it out of you."

The young man looked crestfallen, his shoulders slumping.

"A man was here looking for you."

"For me?"

"Well," the clerk said, "he didn't ask for you by name, but later I realized what he was doing."

"And what was he doing?"

"He flummoxed me."

"Flummoxed?"

"Made a fool of me," the man said. "Got me to tell him your name."

"Wait a minute," Clint said. "Try explaining this to me slower."

"Yes, sir."

After a few minutes Clint understood what had happened.

"Don't feel bad," Clint said. "There are other ways he could have found out who I am."

"Thank you, Mr. Adams," the clerk said, "but I guess that don't make me feel better about bein' fooled."

"I understand," Clint said.

"What should I say if the man comes back?"

"I don't think he'll be coming back. He'll know you told me about him."

"But . . . he told me not to."

"But you did anyway," Clint said. "He'll know that. And thanks."

Clint left the desk and walked up to the second floor. He considered stopping at the girls' room, but instead went directly to his.

He'd had the feeling once or twice that they were being

watched, but his attention had mostly been on seeing that the Shaughnessy sisters got what they wanted, and needed. Now he realized they might have been followed, all the way from New York—even from the docks.

He went to the window and looked down at the front of the hotel. There were people walking by in all directions, but he didn't see anyone who might have simply been watching the hotel.

He went to his bag, took out the curled-up gun and holster, uncurled it, and strapped it on.

TWELVE

Clint went back down to the front of the hotel to take a better look.

"Can I help you with something, sir?" the doorman asked.

"Huh? Oh, no," Clint said. "I just thought I saw someone I know, from my window. Have you seen anyone watching the hotel?"

"Watching?"

"Yes," Clint said, "not coming in, or going out, just standing and . . . watching."

"No, sir," the doorman said. "Nobody like that."

"Okay," Clint said, "thank you."

He went back inside, up to the second floor, and knocked on the door of the Shaughnessy sisters. It was answered by Bridget.

"Are you both all right?" he asked.

She looked at him, at the gun on his hip, then said, "Yes, we are fine."

"Do you need anything?"

"No," she said, "nothing . . . not yet."

"Well, I'll be in my room for the rest of the night," Clint said, "if you need me."

"That is good to know," she said. "Good night."

She closed the door and he went to his own room.

Kemper looked up as Ahern came into the room.

"About time," he said. "I'm starvin'. Can we go eat?"

"Yes," Ahern said, "let's go."

They went out of the hotel and down the street to a greasy café. When they had tough steaks in front of them, Kemper asked, "So? Did you hear?"

"I did," Ahern said. "We got more money."

"How much more?"

"A lot," Ahern said. "Enough to hire help."

"What kind of help?"

"Cheap help," Ahern said.

"Are cheap guns gonna be enough to take care of the Gunsmith?"

"Enough of them will be," Ahern said.

"And where do we get these guns?" Kemper asked. "In Saint Louis?"

"No," Ahern said, "we'll wait 'til we get to Council Bluffs—or maybe even further west."

"How many?"

"I don't know," Ahern said. "We're gettin' the money in advance, sent tomorrow."

"We gotta pick it up?"

Ahern nodded. "A money transfer at a Western Union office."

"But . . . what if Adams and the women leave first thing in the mornin'?"

"Then you'll follow while I get the money," Ahern said. "I'll catch up."

"What if he sees me?"

"He won't," Ahern said. "You don't have to follow that close. We know they're goin' to Council Bluffs from here."

"How do we know that?"

"Because they gotta go that way," Ahern said. "Just follow their trail. Don't get too close."

"Yeah, okay."

"Anyway," Ahern said, "we'll know more in the mornin'. Right now let's just eat."

"You don't have to tell me twice," Kemper said. "They make some good steaks in the West."

THIRTEEN

In the morning Clint rose, dressed, and looked out his window. The team and covered wagon were there with Eclipse tied to the back. He knew they'd be there waiting for him, according to his instructions.

He left his room and walked to the next door, then knocked.

"Hungry?" he asked when Bridget answered.

"Yes, we are."

"We'll have breakfast in the hotel," Clint said. "Then we can get under way."

"Is our wagon here?"

"It is."

"We must get our bags loaded—"

"I'll have the hotel do that while we eat," Clint said.

She nodded and said, "I will fetch my sister."

She closed the door. He waited. After a few moments it opened and both girls stepped out.

"Good morning, Bride," he said.

The younger girl looked at him, smiled, and said, "Good morning, Clint."

They went down to the hotel dining room, stopping first at the front desk to have their bags loaded onto the wagon.

The girls had already seen Clint eat steak and eggs for breakfast along the way, so they both ordered the same. While they ate, they talked to each other, which was fine with Clint. He remained alert, watching the other diners to see if anyone was paying them special attention. He didn't see anyone, however.

"Clint?" Bridget said.

Clint looked at her.

"How long will it take us to get to Council Bluffs?" she asked.

"It's about seven hundred miles," Clint said. "It'll probably take about a month or so. Along the way you'll see a lot of Missouri. We'll stop in Saint Joe, where the Pony Express originated."

"I know the Pony Express," Bride said suddenly. "I read about it."

"You did?" Bridget asked.

"I read a lot about the West."

"Well," Bridget said, "along the way you will have to tell me about what you read."

Ahern and Kemper walked to the Magnolia Hotel and saw the wagon out front.

"Okay," Ahern said. "They're gettin' ready to leave. Get yourself a horse and follow behind them."

"Yeah, okay."

"I'll go and get the money and catch up to you."

"You gonna get us some supplies?"

"Just enough for us to carry, yeah," Ahern said. "All you gotta do is not lose their trail."

"I thought you said we knew where they were going," Kemper asked.

"We do," Ahern said, "but I wanna make sure."

"Yeah, okay," Kemper said again. "But I'll tell you one thing."

"What's that?"

"If he spots me," Kemper said, "I'm lightin' out. I ain't facin' the Gunsmith."

"Yeah, okay, Kemp," Ahern said. "Just don't let him see you."

"Yeah, right."

When they'd finished their breakfast, Clint accompanied the ladies out to the wagon. They were both wearing skirts, but when they arrived in Council Bluffs—or even along the way—he was going to have them buy some britches.

"What about supplies?" Bride asked when they reached the wagon. "I read that you need a lot of supplies to travel by wagon."

"Don't worry," Clint said. "I had my friend stock us up with them."

"What a beautiful horse," Bridget said, looking at Eclipse.

"Yes, he is."

"He looks like an Irish breed," she said.

"Arabian," Clint said.

"Are you sure?"

He smiled.

"Yes, I'm sure."

He helped both women onto the wagon, Bride in the back, and Bridget up front with him.

"Bridget, there is more room back here than you would think," she said. "This will not be so bad."

Clint didn't say anything. He wondered how many days it would be before she changed her mind.

FOURTEEN

By the middle of the first day, Bride wanted to change places with Bridget. Clint stopped the wagon so they could change places. He was afraid if he kept moving, one of them would fall off. Maybe later, after they'd traveled for a few days, they'd be more used to the movements of the wagon and be able to change places without stopping.

The constant motion was hard for them to get used to, and the dust they kicked up bothered them to the point where Clint had them tie kerchiefs around their mouths. What they did enjoy about the trip right from the beginning was the scenery.

While Bride was sitting up front with him, she finally loosened up enough to start talking to him.

"What about Indians?" she asked.

"What about them?"

"Will we see any?"

"Maybe."

"Will they attack us?"

"Probably not."

"But I read that they are bloodthirsty."

"There was a time when they were," Clint said, "but there aren't that many Indians right now off the reservations."

"Oh." She seemed disappointed. "What about outlaws?"

"Oh, there are still a lot of outlaws."

"Will they attack us?"

"I hope not."

"But if they do, you'll shoot them, right?"

"If I have to."

They rode in silence for a while after that, and just when he thought she had asked enough questions, she asked, "Will you teach me to shoot?"

"Why do you want to learn how to shoot?"

"To defend myself," she said. "And my sister."

"Bride, I think it would be up to your husband to teach you to shoot."

"Yes," she said quietly, "my husband."

That thought didn't seem to make her very happy.

"But," she said after a few moments, "he is a miner. You are the Gunsmith. Wouldn't it be better if you taught me?"

"We have a long way to go," Clint told her. "We'll see."

The same thing parents told their kids when they asked for some rock candy.

After a while Bridget stuck her head between them and asked, "Will we be stopping to eat soon?"

"We have about an hour of daylight left," Clint told her. "We'll stop then."

"I found some sort of hard meat back here."

"Beef jerky," Clint said. "You can chew on that if you like."

"Beef jerky?" Bride asked.

"It's dried beef."

"Oh, beef!" Bride said excitedly. "Bridget, may I have a piece?"

Bridget withdrew her head, then reappeared and gave Clint and Bride each a piece, and kept one for herself.

Bride took a bite, yanked and yanked until a piece came off in her mouth, and then chewed enthusiastically.

"It's very good," she said.

"A little chewy," Bridget said.

"I don't care," Bride said. "It is better than potatoes."

Clint had always thought what he'd heard about the Irish and potatoes was a myth, but in listening to these two girls, and watching them eat, apparently that wasn't the case.

"Won't be any potatoes on this trip," Clint said. "And that's probably the only beef you'll be getting."

"Won't we be eating when we stop?" Bride asked.

"Yes, we will."

"In a restaurant?"

"No," Clint said. "For most of this trip we'll be making camp on the trail, and eating over an open fire."

"Where will we sleep?" she asked.

"On the ground," Clint said."

"What if it rains?"

"Then under the wagon," he said, "or in it."

Bride gave her sister an outraged look, but Bridget didn't say anything.

"Hey," Clint said, "you girls wanted to see the way we live in the West."

"What will we eat?"

"Bacon and beans," Clint said, "for as long as it lasts."

"B-But . . . what if we run out of food?" Bride asked.

"We'll try not to," Clint said. "We'll restock when we do come to a town."

Bride apparently decided to stop asking questions she didn't like the answers to, and stared off into the distance.

FIFTEEN

As darkness began to fall, they camped. Clint dispatched the girls to find firewood while he took care of the horses.

"Make sure it's something that will burn," he said.

They returned with an armful each, and he built a fire and then put on a pot of coffee. After that he took out a frying pan for the bacon and beans.

As they sat around the fire, Clint noticed that Bride kept looking around, as if expecting to be attacked at any moment.

"I assume you ladies didn't spend much time in Ireland sleeping outside."

"We may not have had much," Bridget said, "but we did usually have a roof over our heads, and a bed of sorts."

"Well, there's nothing to be worried about," Clint said.

"What about animals?" Bride asked.

"They won't come near the fire."

"And outlaws?" she asked. "What if they sneak up on us while we sleep?"

"They won't be able to sneak up, because I'll be watching."

"All night?" she asked.

"Yes," he said.

That didn't seem to soothe her very much.

"Here," he said, "concentrate on this." He handed each girl a plate of bacon and beans, and then offered them a cup of coffee.

"I don't like coffee," Bride said. "Don't we have some tea?"

"No tea," Clint said. "You can drink water from the canteen."

Bridget accepted the coffee, but not Bride. She morosely began to eat her food.

"This is very good," Bridget proclaimed.

"It's trail food," Clint said. "I like trail food a lot."

"Is this what they eat on trail drives?" Bridget asked. Her sister looked at her. "I read about them," Bridget explained.

"Sometimes," Clint said, "but on a trail drive they have a chuck wagon and a cook with them, so they eat other things."

"Like what?" Bride asked.

"Soup, stew, some beef if a cow happened to be butchered."

"I wish we had a chuck wagon," Bride said.

"Hey," Clint said, "I'm considered to be a pretty good trail cook."

That didn't seem to impress Bride.

"You ladies have your choice," he said. "You can sleep inside the wagon, or out under the stars."

"I will sleep in the wagon," Bride said quickly.

"I will sleep under the stars," Bridget said.

"Good," Clint said to her.

Bride finished her food and set her plate aside, but Bridget extended her plate to Clint for seconds. Clint wondered how Bride was going to do when she was living with Ed O'Neil at his gold mining camp. Maybe his old friend would build a house for her.

When they'd finished, Clint showed Bridget how to clean the plates and cups using dirt. Bride got up and went to the wagon, climbing inside. She was moving around in there for a while, probably getting her bedding set up, and then the wagon stopped rocking.

As instructed by Ahern, Kemper had made a cold camp when he stopped for the night. His supper was beef jerky and water. Thankfully, the fall night was mild.

He was just starting to drift off to sleep when he heard someone approaching the camp. He drew his gun, got up into a crouch, and waited.

"Hello, the camp," Ahern's voice came from the darkness, just loud enough to be heard.

"That you, Ahern?" Kemper asked.

"It's me."

"Come ahead."

Kemper entered the camp on foot, leading his horse.

"Why didn't you make a fire?" he asked.

"You told me to make a cold camp."

"You're upwind, Kemp," Ahern said. He sniffed the air. "All Adams is gonna smell is his own coffee and bacon. Make a fire, I brought some beans."

"You don't got to tell me twice."

Once they had a fire going, and were eating beans and drinking coffee, Kemper said, "You got our money?"

"I got it."

"Lemme see it."

"What for?" Ahern asked.

"I just wanna see it."

"Later," Ahern said. "It's in my saddlebags."

"How much?"

"Enough," Ahern said. "Enough to do the job. How far ahead of us are they camped?"

"About a mile."

"That's too close," Ahern said. "Tomorrow night we'll fall back further."

"We don't wanna lose 'em."

"We won't lose 'em."

"What about when we get to Council Bluffs, and after?" Kemper asked. "When we head west? Neither one of us can track."

"By then we'll have somebody with us who can," Ahern said. "Don't worry. I was late gettin' here because I took the time to send a few more telegrams."

"To who?"

"Don't worry about it," Ahern said. "Just know that when we get to Council Bluffs, we'll be all set. We'll have everything we need to get the job done."

"I hope so," Kemper said.

"I'm tellin' you so, Kemp," Ahern said. "Just believe me."

SIXTEEN

True to her word, Bridget slept outside, under the stars, wrapped in a blanket. During the night Clint could see the wagon moving as Bride was tossing and turning.

He hadn't lied about being on watch all night. He was concerned about being followed from Saint Louis so he intended to stay on watch with his rifle across his knees. Anytime he might have dozed, he could depend on Eclipse to alert him to any trouble.

Halfway through the night he noticed Bridget turn over and toss off her blanket. She got to her feet, straightened her skirt, and then came over to him by the fire.

"Do you mind if I sit?" she asked.

"Not at all," he said. "Would you like some coffee?"

"Please."

He poured her a cup and handed it to her.

"Thank you."

He nodded, drank from his own cup. He stared straight out into the darkness.

"How do you do this?" she asked.

"Do what?"

"Keep watch," she said. "Not sleep?"

"It's not hard," he said. "My body is still at rest while I sit here."

"Do you stare into the dark all night?"

"Oh yes," he said. "If you look into the fire, it destroys your night vision. If someone—or something—comes at you in that moment, you won't see them."

"I understand," she said. Then she added, " 'Something'?"

"A wolf," he said, "or a big cat. They don't usually come near a fire, but sometimes . . ."

"Sometimes what?"

"Sometimes they get hungry enough . . . I didn't want to worry your sister."

"So you decided to worry me instead?" she asked with raised eyebrows.

He looked at her.

"You're stronger," he said. "I suspect that's why you came with her to meet her prospective husband."

"I came with her because we are family," she said, "the only family we have."

"Does Ed know you're coming along?"

"He does," she said. "We made it a condition."

"Oh, of course," Clint said. "He told me in the letter I'd be meeting two ladies."

"You appeared to be very surprised when you saw us," she said. "You were expecting two older women, weren't you?"

"I was," he said. "Ed is . . . well, I'm sure you know he's over sixty."

"We know," she said. "But we wanted to get out of Ireland, and he sent the fare money."

"Did it ever occur to you to go your own way when you got to this country?"

"I'll not lie, Clint," she said. "'Twas more than a passing thought. But we cannot do that."

"Too honest?"

She laughed.

"Too frightened."

He laughed then.

"I admire your honesty."

She put her hand on his arm.

"May I continue to be honest?"

"Please."

Now she gave his arm a squeeze.

"I find you very attractive," she said. "I did from the moment I saw you."

"I'm flattered."

"Are you attracted to me?"

"Very much so," he said. "You're lovely."

She removed her hand from his arm, put it on his thigh.

"I almost approached you on the train, and again in the hotel," she said.

"What stopped you?"

She smiled and removed her hand from his body completely.

"Bride," she said. "She made me promise . . . I had a wild period in my youth, Clint."

"Your youth?"

"My teens," she said. "I was . . . a rebel. Our parents were very religious, and I rebelled against that. Bride made me promise I'd never do that again."

"I see."

"But it wouldn't be that . . . with you," she said. "I know that."

She leaned closer to him, and he did the same. They kissed, gently at first, and then the kiss deepened until Clint pulled away.

"Another time and place, Bridget," he said.

"Yes," she said. "I wouldn't want Bride—"

At that moment the wagon began to rock again.

"She can't get comfortable," he said.

"Give her time."

"You know," he said, "you won't be living in great

comfort in Shasta. I mean . . . it is a mining camp you're going to."

"We know that," she said, "but it will still be better than where we were."

"I hope so."

She pressed her cheek to his shoulder, then said, "I better get back to sleep. I'll see you in the morning."

"Early," Clint said. "I'll have some breakfast ready."

"I look forward to it," she said, "and a lot more."

She went back to her bedroll and wrapped herself up in her blanket. Clint could still taste her on his lips, and he recalled the freckles on her chest. He wondered how far down they went.

Kemper stared out into the darkness, wondering why he had to stand watch. After all, they weren't being followed; they were doing the following. Ahern snored from his bedroll, and Kemper poured himself another cup of coffee.

SEVENTEEN

Clint had a fresh pot of coffee ready when the girls woke up, and some strips of bacon. He had to go to the wagon and give it a shake to wake Bride, who—after tossing and turning most of the night—seemed to have settled down.

"Time to get up," he called. "Breakfast is ready."

"I'm coming," she moaned.

Clint turned and walked to the fire, found Bridget waiting there for him.

"I must warn you, Bride is not a morning person."

"That's okay," he said. "I've ridden with few people who are."

"Here she comes."

Bride climbed down from the wagon, stumbled a bit on the way to the fire. Bridget handed her a cup of coffee.

"I did not sleep very well," she complained.

"You'll get used to it," Clint said. "Here, have some bacon."

She accepted the plate, and sat down at the fire.

"Will we be getting to a town today?" she asked.

"Probably not," Clint said. "Unless we come across a small one I'm not aware of."

"There must be many towns in the West you are not aware of," she observed.

"I'm sure there are."

That seemed to make her more hopeful.

When they were finished with breakfast, Clint said, "If you ladies will clean up, I'll take care of getting the horses ready."

"Yes, we'll do so," Bridget said.

"Okay, thanks. And make sure the fire is out. Pour the rest of the coffee on it, and then kick it until it's out."

As Clint walked away, Bridget noticed Bride looking at her strangely.

"What did you do?" Bride asked when Clint was out of earshot.

"What do you mean?"

"You know what I mean, dear sister," Bride said.

"I did not do anything, Bride," Bridget said.

"Is that the truth?"

"It is," Bridget said. "Do you want me to swear on the Bible?"

"I do not want you to swear," Bride said archly. "I believe you."

"Fine. Let's clean up, then."

"With dirt?"

"Yes," Bridget said, "with dirt."

A mile behind them another camp was breaking for the day.

"Did you get any tobacco?" Kemper asked.

"I did." He passed his partner some tobacco and paper.

"Can I smoke?" Kemper asked.

"We're still upwind," Ahern said. "Go ahead."

Ahern finished kicking the fire to death, then went to saddle his horse. Kemper made a cigarette, lit it, and started saddling his own horse.

"Why don't we go ahead of them?" he asked.

"What?" Ahern asked.

"If we know where they're going," Kemper asked, "why don't we circle ahead of them?"

Ahern turned and looked at his friend.

"What?" Kemper asked.

"I was just thinking," Ahern said, "that might be the first time you've ever had a good idea."

"Maybe it's just the first time you ever listened to what I have to say."

Ahern thought a moment, then said, "No, that's not it."

EIGHTEEN

They traveled several more days without stopping at a town.
Clint finally relented and pulled into the town of Calvert. It
had a general store that doubled as a saloon, and not much
else. They restocked a bit but the ladies were not able to find
a bathtub. They did, however, buy several pairs of britches.

After they left town, the girls took turns in the back of
the wagon, changing from their skirts to their pants. When
they were done, Bridget ended up in front with Clint, while
Bride was in the back of the wagon.

She noticed Clint craning his neck to look back behind
them, and she put her hand on his arm. He whipped his head
around to look at her.

"Is something wrong?" she asked.

"I'm just keeping an eye out behind us," he said.

"Do you think we're being followed?"

"Well, maybe not followed," he said.

"What do you mean?"

"I mean I thought someone might be trailing us—that
is, not following us, but following our trail, keeping out of
sight."

"Why would they do that?"

"I don't know," he said. "They could be following me

because they recognized me, and at some point, they may want to try me."

"Try you?"

"Try to kill me."

"Why?"

"Just because of who I am."

"That must be a terrible thing to live with," she said.

"On the other hand," he said, "maybe it's not me."

"What do you mean?" she asked.

"Is there any reason you and your sister might have been followed?"

"From Ireland?"

"I don't know," he said. "From Ireland, from New York."

"Why would anyone follow us?" she asked.

"I don't know," he said. "I'm asking you."

"I have no idea."

"Well," Clint said with one last look behind them, "maybe I'm just wrong."

Ahern and Kemper rode into Saint Joseph, Missouri, ahead of Clint and the Shaughnessy sisters.

"Why don't we wait for them here?" Kemper asked when they stopped in a saloon for a drink.

"No," Ahern said.

"Why not?"

"Because I've already made plans for Council Bluffs," he said. "I've got some men waitin' for us there."

"Oh," Kemper said. "Well, why didn't you tell me that before?"

"I didn't think there was any reason to confuse you."

"Why do you always treat me like I'm stupid?"

"Seems to me I'm less likely to make a mistake that way," Ahern said.

"What?"

"Never mind," Ahern said. "Drink your beer, then we'll pick up some coffee and jerky and get back on the trail."

"Why don't we spend the night?"

"Why don't you stop makin' suggestions, Kemp?" Ahern asked.

"Hey," Kemper said, "I'm the one who suggested we get ahead of them, remember?"

"Yeah," Ahern said, "and you should quit while you're ahead."

NINETEEN

When they rode into Saint Joseph, Bride was visibly relieved to see a real town.

"The first thing I want is a bathtub," she said, "and a hot bath."

They had bathed along the way in streams and water-holes, but they were all cold, just a quick in and out.

"I want a long soak," Bridget said.

They both looked at Clint.

"All right," he said, "we'll stay overnight in a hotel and you can have your baths."

Bridget leaned over and sniffed him audibly.

"You could use one, too, you know."

She and Bride both giggled.

Clint stopped at the first hotel they came to. He went inside with them, registered them all, and arranged for their baths.

"I'm going to take care of the horses," Clint said, "and put our wagon in a safe place. Don't leave the hotel, all right?"

"Why?" Bride asked. "Is this a dangerous town?"

"I just want to know where you are," Clint said. "You're my responsibility."

"We'll stay," Bridget said. "You go and do what you have to do."

He left the hotel and drove the wagon to the livery stable. He made arrangements with the man there to care for the three horses, and watch over the wagon. He promised to lock his place up at night, with the wagon inside. Clint paid him half the agreed-upon amount in advance.

He walked back to the hotel, keeping a sharp eye out for anyone suspicious. He reached the building without seeing anyone who was paying him any special attention.

Inside he arranged with the clerk for a bath of his own, then got his key and went to his room, which was across the hall from the sisters.

He left his bag and rifle on the bed, then walked across to their door and knocked.

Bride answered.

"Everything okay?" he asked.

"Yes," she said. "Bridget is in the bath. When she comes back, I will go."

"Okay," he said. "I'm right across the hall, if you need anything."

"We will, Clint. Thank you."

He went back to his own room, figured to wait until both girls were finished with their baths before taking one himself.

Owen Brown owned and ran the livery stable, but he also had another part-time job—as a deputy. After Clint Adams left his stable, he locked up and walked to the sheriff's office.

Sheriff Cargill looked up as Owen entered and said, "Your not due to be on duty for another day, Owen."

"I know that, Steve," Brown said. "I just thought I ought to tell you who was just at my stable."

"Oh? Who's that?" Cargill was still staring at something on his desk as he asked.

"Clint Adams."

Cargill's head jerked up.

"The Gunsmith?"

"That's right."

"What's he doing in Saint Joe?"

"He didn't say," Brown answered, "but he's got a wagon with him. Left it at my place with his horse, and team."

"What's in the wagon?"

"I didn't look."

The sheriff stood up and grabbed his hat.

"Well, let's have a look now," he said, "before I go and talk to him."

"He ain't done nothin', Sheriff."

"He's in town, Owen. That can't be good. You know that, or you wouldn't be here."

"I'm just tryin' to be a good deputy, Sheriff."

"You are, Owen," the sheriff said. "You are. Now, come on. Show me that wagon."

Clint heard the door to the girls' room open and close, assumed Bridget had come back. Then it opened and closed again. Bride going for her bath. When it opened and closed again, that would be his cue to go down for his own bath. All he had to do until then was relax, and wait his turn.

He took off his gun belt, hung it on the bedpost, sat on the bed, and decided not to remove his boots. He reclined on the bed with his hands locked behind his head, and stared at the ceiling.

Sometime later he heard the floor creaking in the hall. He was reclining on the bed, waiting for his turn with the bathtub. He grabbed his gun and moved to the door. The footsteps were too heavy to belong to either one of the girls.

He stood at the door with his left hand on the knob, his gun in his right. Abruptly, there was a knock on the door, which surprised him. He opened it, saw a man with a badge standing in the hall. He was tall, very thin, with a lock of gray hair hanging down from beneath his hat.

"You won't need that," the man said. "I'm the law."

"I see the badge," Clint said.

"I earned it in an election," the man said. "You wanna come down to the lobby and ask the desk clerk?"

Clint thought a moment, then said, "No. You want to come in, or you want me to come out?"

"In is okay," the sheriff said. "I just wanna talk."

Clint backed away from the door and said, "Come on in, Sheriff."

TWENTY

"My name is Sheriff Steve Cargill," the lawman said. "I got word you were in town, kinda made me curious."

"So you took a look at my wagon already, right?" Clint asked. Instead of returning his gun to the holster on the bedpost, he tucked it into his belt.

"I did."

"The man at the livery?"

"Owen is also a part-time deputy."

"Ah."

"Were you gonna come and see me?"

"I would have," Clint said, "if I was going to be in town past tomorrow morning."

"So you're just passin' through?"

"Literally," Clint said. "I'm on my way to Council Bluffs."

"Travelin' alone?"

"No, I've got two young ladies with me."

"Whores?" Cargill asked with a frown.

"No," Clint said, without taking offense, "I haven't taken up pimping. They're a couple of sisters from Ireland who want to see the country on their way to Shasta County, California."

"What are they gonna do there?"

"One of them is getting married," Clint said. "The other one is her sister."

"Mail-order bride?"

"Something like that."

"That's not your usual kind of job, is it?"

"It's not a job," Clint said, "it's a favor."

"That's a lot of time to put in for a favor," the sheriff said. He was still trying to figure out if Clint was lying to him or not.

"Sheriff," Clint said, "there's nothing here in Saint Joe that interests me. Believe me, we're moving on in the morning."

"Uh-huh."

"I don't blame you for being suspicious."

"That's my job."

"I know it," Clint said. "I take no offense that you went through my wagon. You didn't find anything unusual, did you?"

"No," Cargill said.

"Well, there you go," Clint said.

"Okay," Cargill said "I'm gonna take your word for it—for now. But if you don't leave in the mornin', I'm gonna wanna know why."

"Agreed."

"Good night, then."

"Good night, Sheriff."

The lawman opened the door and stepped out into the hall, leaving the door ajar. As Clint went to close it, the door across the hall opened and Bridget peered out.

"Is everything all right?" she asked.

"Everything's fine," Clint said. "I just got a visit from the local law."

"May I . . ." she said, hesitating.

"Come right in," Clint said.

Bridget left her room, closing the door behind her, and entered Clint's room.

"What did he want?" she asked as Clint shut and locked his door.

"What all lawmen want when I ride into their town," he said. "They want to know why."

"What did you tell him?"

"Exactly why we're here," Clint said. "And that we'll be leaving first thing in the morning."

"What did he say?"

"What could he say?" Clint asked. "He's still suspicious. He'll watch us in the morning to make sure we go."

"I see."

She turned and looked at the door, then glanced at the bed.

"Bride is taking her bath."

"I know. I'm waiting my turn."

"Oh?"

"Didn't you say I needed one?"

"I understood that Western men bathed infrequently . . . if at all."

"I'm well acquainted with bathtubs. I've been known to use one, say, two or maybe three times . . . a year."

She laughed.

"I had intended to try to seduce you while Bride was bathing," she said, "but maybe I'll wait until you're clean."

"That sounds like a plan," Clint said, "but what will you tell Bride?"

"Perhaps," she said, moving toward the door, "I'll simply wait until she is asleep. After all those nights in the wagon, she'll probably sleep very soundly."

She went out, closing the door gently behind her. Clint wondered if she was actually telling him the truth, and if he should expect her during the night.

TWENTY-ONE

Clint heard Bride return from her bath. He cracked his door to make sure, watched her enter the room she was sharing with her sister. He stepped into the hall and went down to the front desk.

"Is anyone using the bath?" he asked.

"No, sir," the man said, "a young lady has just vacated it. Shall I have it prepared for you?"

"Yes," Clint said. "Hot."

"Wait here," the clerk said. "I'll make the arrangements, and get you some towels."

"Thank you."

The clerk was back in a few minutes, said, "It's all ready. Just walk straight back to the last door on the right."

"Thanks."

Clint took the towels and went down the hall.

Refreshed from his bath, Clint left the hotel to go and check on the wagon. He had told the lawman he didn't mind having the wagon searched, but he did want to make sure that everything that was supposed to be there was still there. He also wanted to check on the horses, especially Eclipse.

The streets were still busy, as darkness had not yet fallen. When he reached the stable, the doors were open and he walked right in. The man the sheriff had called Owen saw him and stood up straight, dropped the leg of the horse he'd been inspecting.

"Mr. Adams," he said, "I—I didn't—"

"Relax, Owen," Clint said. "I know you spoke to the sheriff. It's fine."

"It is?"

"You're a part-time deputy, right?"

"Yessir."

"Then you were just doing your job."

"Yessir."

"We don't have a problem," Clint said. "I just wanted to check on my animals, and get something out of my wagon."

"Go right ahead, sir."

Of course, there was nothing he needed from the wagon; he just wanted to make sure everything was there.

He took a look at the team first, found them to be standing easily, feeding. Then he looked in on Eclipse, who was also feeding. Next, he went to the wagon and climbed in back. Out of sight he made a complete search, found that everything was there, although it was obvious that some of the girls' bags had been opened. He had no idea what the sheriff might have found—or might have expected to find—that would have caused him concern. Of course, there had been nothing.

He came out of the wagon, unmindful of the fact that he wasn't carrying anything. He didn't care if Owen noticed.

"Everything okay, sir?" the man asked.

"Everything is fine, Owen," Clint said. "Just fine. Make sure you tell the sheriff I was here."

"Oh, uh, yes, well, okay, sir."

"Good night."

"Night, Mr. Adams."

Clint left the livery stable and walked back to the hotel.

Owen Brown let out the breath he was holding, briefly thought of going to the sheriff's office, then decided nothing had really happened that he needed to report on.

But he sure could use a drink.

TWENTY-TWO

Owen went to the Red Garter Saloon and started drinking whiskey. After a few shots he began talking about the Gunsmith being in Saint Joseph. This caught the attention of three men sitting at a table, sharing a bottle of whiskey. They decided to invite Owen to their table to buy him a few more drinks.

Owen's head was on the table half an hour later.

"He's out," Fred Doolin said, leaning over to check.

"You think he's tellin' the truth?" Ames Connor asked.

"Why would he lie?" Denny Scott asked. "If the Gunsmith is in town, he's in town."

"Jesus," Fred said, "you know what it means to the man who kills Clint Adams?"

"A rep," Ames said.

"A big rep," Denny said.

The three men exchanged an anxious glance.

"How do we do it without gettin' killed?" Ames asked.

"We plan it," Denny said, "very carefully."

Clint got back to his room as it was getting dark. He went to the window and looked down at the street. The sheriff was still the only person in town who had taken any interest in him.

He was still staring out the window when there was a light knock on his door. He doubted that Bride had fallen fast asleep yet. His own stomach was growling, so the girls must have been hungry by now.

He answered the door and Bridget said, "Can we go and eat?"

"You girls eat a lot," Clint said.

"Traveling with you builds up an appetite," Bridget said. Across the hall, Bride was standing in the open doorway and she nodded her agreement.

"We'll just go down to the hotel dining room," he said. "I'm sure the sheriff would like me to stay out of trouble."

"That's fine," Bridget said. "We've been eating your bacon and beans for days."

"Let me guess," he said, pulling his door closed. "Time for a steak?"

Fred, Ames, and Denny left Owen Brown with his head on the table as they went outside for some air.

"What do we do?" Ames asked. "We know what hotel he's in. Do we wanna surprise him? Or wait until he comes out?"

"You wanna face him fair and square in the street?" Denny asked.

"I don't," Fred said before Ames could reply.

"No," Ames said, "I don't either."

"Okay," Denny said, "then we're better off takin' him in his room. We'll wait 'til it's late, so he's asleep."

"We gonna kill 'im while he's asleep?" Fred asked. "How's that gonna give us a big reputation?"

"Nobody's gonna care how he got killed," Denny said. "The headline's just gonna say 'Gunsmith Killed.'"

"Denny's right," Ames said, "this is our best chance."

Fred looked worried.

"What is it?" Denny asked.

"I ain't never killed nobody before."

"Don't worry about it," Denny said. "The first one's the hardest."

TWENTY-THREE

They finished eating and returned to their rooms.

"Are you girls satisfied now?" Clint asked in the hall.

"Well . . ." Bride said.

"What is it?" Clint asked.

"Tomorrow we go back to bacon and beans," she lamented.

"I tell you what," Clint said. "When we get to Council Bluffs, I'll buy some cans of fruit, and the makings for some biscuits for the trip west."

The two girls didn't look thrilled.

"Hey," Clint said, "at least that'll give us a little more variety."

"Good night, Clint," Bride said, entering her room.

"Night, Bride."

Bridget gave him a look and said, "Yes, good night, Clint."

The look in her eyes wasn't saying good night, though.

"Hey, can you help me?" the man asked.

The clerk looked up from what he was doing at the man who had just entered the hotel lobby.

"What?"

"I need some help out here," Ames said. Of the three compadres, Ames was the one who was unknown to this particular desk clerk.

"What's the matter?"

"There's somethin' happenin' in the alley out here, next to your hotel," Ames said. "You're gonna wanna know about it."

The clerk came around the desk and approached Ames, frowning.

"What do you mean?"

"Well, come out here and I'll show ya," Ames said.

"I'm not supposed to leave the lobby."

"It'll take a minute," Ames said. "Two, at the most."

"Well . . . okay," the clerk said. "Show me."

"Come on."

Ames led the way and the clerk left the lobby.

As soon as they were gone, Fred and Denny entered.

"Stay by the door," Denny said. "Lemme know if anybody's comin'."

Denny ran behind the desk, opened the register, and ran his finger over the names until he came to the one he wanted.

"Got it?" Fred asked.

"I got it," Denny said. "The Gunsmith is in Room 15."

"Let's get out of here!" Fred said.

Denny joined Fred at the door and the two men left. Moments later the clerk came in, shaking his head and talking to himself.

"Crazy sonofabitch," he said, getting back behind the desk. "Callin' me outside for no reason. Damn it."

Nothing was amiss in the lobby or behind the desk, so he went back to work.

The door to the sheriff's office slammed open and two men entered, dragging a third man between them.

"What happened?" Sheriff Cargill asked.

"Owen got a snoutful, that's what happened," one of the

men said. Cargill knew his name was Paul. He didn't know the other man. "The barkeep said we should bring him here so he could sleep it off."

"Damn it," Cargill said. "He's not wearin' his badge, is he?"

"Don't think so," the other man said. "Coulda fell off, though."

"That's all I need," Cargill said. "Put him on a cot in one of the cells."

They dragged him into the cell block, dropped him in one of the cells, and came out.

"What was he doin' there?" Cargill asked.

"He came in and started drinkin', then started tellin' wild tales."

"What kind of tales?"

"Oh, somethin' about the Gunsmith bein' in Saint Joe," Paul said.

"Crazy talk," the other man said.

"Yeah," Cargill said, "crazy."

"We gotta go," Paul said.

"Thanks for bringin' him in."

"Sure, Sheriff."

After the two men left, Cargill went into the cell block and looked down at his snoring deputy. He wondered if anyone in the saloon had believed Owen about Clint Adams being in town.

That would definitely be trouble.

TWENTY-FOUR

Clint wasn't happy.

He'd hoped to get in and out of Saint Joe without anyone knowing he was there. Now not only did the sheriff know, but his part-time deputy as well. If one if them talked, the word would get around, and there was always—without exception, no matter what town he was in—always someone who wanted to try him. And as the years went by, it did not become easier. Each time he survived, his reputation got bigger, so the next time they came at him not by ones and twos, but by threes and sixes.

He lay on his bed, with his holster hanging by his head. All he needed was to get through the night, and get out of town.

Just one night.

Was that too much to ask?

"Okay," Denny said in the Red Garter, "we know what room he's in. Now all we gotta do is wait until he's asleep, and then go in and get him."

"We gonna go in the back?" Fred asked.

"No," Denny said, "we'll go right in the front."

"What about the clerk?" Ames asked.

"He won't do anythin'," Denny said. "He won't have time. We'll go right up the stairs and get it done."

"What about the sheriff?" Fred asked.

"What about him?" Denny asked.

"What do we tell him?" Ames asked. "He's gonna show up, you know."

"We'll deal with him when the time comes," Denny said. "Once the Gunsmith is dead, what's he gonna do anyway?"

"I—I dunno," Ames said.

"Just relax," Denny said. "Let me do the thinkin' and the talkin'."

"So when do we go?" Fred asked.

"When I say so," Denny said. "Fred, why don't you get us another beer?"

"Huh? Oh yeah, sure."

After Fred went to the bar, Denny asked, "You think he'll pull the trigger?"

"Huh? Oh, sure, why not? Oh, you mean because of what he said? Naw, he's ready. Don't worry."

"I'm not worried," Denny said, "but if he doesn't do his part, I'll kill him right after we kill the Gunsmith."

Ames looked over at Fred, returning with three beers, and said, "That's okay with me."

TWENTY-FIVE

Clint was alert for the sounds of the floorboards in the hall. There was no access to his room by the window, so he didn't have to worry about that. If they made it through the night, he'd still have to worry about stepping out onto the street in the morning. If someone wanted to make a try for him, that would be the time. They'd either face him in the street, or try to ambush him.

He heard the boards creak, but he had also heard the door to Bridget and Bride's room open. Then there was a knock at his door.

He knew it was her, but still he took the gun with him when he answered it. As he opened the door, she quickly stepped in, the scent of her tickling his nostrils as she came. He closed the door and turned to face her. She was wearing a cotton nightgown that clung to her, making it clear there was nothing underneath. Her nipples were poking into the fabric.

"Bride's asleep," she said. "Fast asleep."

"Really?" he asked. "Even I heard your door creak open."

"Don't worry," she said. "She's asleep."

"Bridget," he said, "this may not be a good idea."

She loosened something on her nightgown, and it fell to

the floor. She was naked, and he could see that the freckles spread over her pert breasts. Her rust-colored nipples were hard. The hair between her legs was an even deeper red than the hair on her head. And the scent of her was . . . womanly.

"Do you want me to go?"

He drank in the sight of her and said, "No."

She smiled, and approached him. She ran her hand down his arm, until it was touching his gun.

"Do we need that?"

"I hope not."

She took the gun from him, walked to the bedpost, and slid it into the holster. Her naked butt was stunning to watch as she walked. There was not an ounce of fat on her body.

She turned, beckoned to him, and said, "Come to bed, Clint."

He started for her, but she stopped him.

"Wait!"

"What?"

"Not with all those clothes on."

Hurriedly, he began to remove them.

"That's his window," Denny said, pointing.

"His light is still burning," Fred pointed out.

"I can see that," Denny said. "We're gonna stand here and wait for it to go out."

"What if it doesn't?"

"It has to go out sometime," Ames said. "He has to go to sleep."

"Right," Denny said, staring at the window from across the street. "Sometime."

Naked, Clint crossed the room to Bridget and took her into his arms.

"I like your freckles," he said.

"Really?" she said. "In Ireland we all have them."

"Well, not here," he said. He bent his head and began to

kiss the freckles. When his mouth came near her nipples, he caught them in his teeth, pulled on them, sucked them into his mouth.

"Oh!" she gasped.

His hands roamed her body, over the smooth skin of her back, down to her buttocks, which he clenched in his hands. He got to his knees in front of her, kissed her belly, moved lower, slid his tongue into the red forest of her pubic thatch so he could taste her.

She gasped and jumped back from him.

"What are you doing?" she demanded.

"No one's ever done that to you before?" he asked. "I thought you said you were wild."

"Not that wild," she said. "That's French stuff."

"And it's very nice," he said.

"You do that here?" she asked. "In the West?"

"Well," he said, "I do." He stood up, put his hand out to her. "Come here."

She came to him. He slid his hand down over her belly, into her crotch, where she was wet. She gasped when his fingers touched her.

"Come to bed," he said into her ear, "and I'll show you."

He tugged her toward the bed, turned her, and laid her down on it.

"Wait," she said.

"Why?"

"The light," she said. "Put the light out."

"All right."

He walked to the lamp on the wall by the door and turned it all the way down, plunging the room into total darkness.

From across the street, the three men saw the light go out.

"That's it," Denny said. "Let's go."

TWENTY-SIX

The clerk looked up as the three men came charging into the lobby.

"What the hell—"

"Shut up!" Denny told him.

"Hey, you!" the clerk said, pointing to Ames. "You're crazy!"

Denny pointed his gun at the clerk and said, "Shut the hell up."

"What the hell—" the clerk said again, but he shut up.

"Don't say another word," Denny said. "Duck down behind your desk and stay there."

"But—"

"Do it!"

The clerk ducked down.

Denny turned to Ames and Fred and said, "Okay, let's go."

"What room?" Fred asked.

"I told you before," Denny said. "Room 15."

In Room 15, Clint had joined Bridget on the bed. In the darkness he reached for her, slid his hands up her legs and thighs, then even higher to her breasts. She sighed as he palmed them, her nipples hard as pebbles against his palms.

He moved up alongside her and kissed her, sliding his hand back down her body until it was between her legs again. This time when he touched her, she started, but did not pull away.

"Oh my," she whispered as he probed. "Oh, glory be . . ."

In the hall the three men crept along quietly, Denny in the lead. They all had their guns in their hands. As they approached Room 15, the door to Room 14 suddenly opened. A sleepy-looking girl appeared, rubbing her eyes and saying, "Bridget?"

The three men froze. The girl saw them, and screamed . . .

"Bride!" Bridget shouted.

Even in the dark, Clint's hand went directly to the butt of his gun. He sprang from the bed and ran to the door. Naked, he yanked the door open and stepped into the hall.

The three men froze when the girl screamed. Denny almost pulled the trigger on her, but managed to restrain himself.

The door to Room 15 opened and a naked man sprang into the hall, gun in hand.

Bride, who had awakened abruptly, became concerned when she didn't see Bridget in bed. She stumbled to the door, rubbing her eyes, and opened the door, calling her sister's name. When she saw the three gunmen in the hall, she couldn't help herself. She screamed.

When she saw the door across the hall open and Clint Adams sprang into the hall, naked, she screamed again . . .

"Jesus!" Fred snapped. He turned and ran back along the hall to the stairway.

Denny and Ames saw Clint, and although stunned, each tried to bring their guns to bear.

Clint, spotting the three gunmen, saw one of them flee, and the other two turned toward him.

He fired.

Bride screamed a third time.

As Clint's slugs struck Denny and Ames, they both pulled the triggers of their guns. Denny fired into the floor, while Ames's bullets went into the ceiling.

Both men went over backward, though, and ended up on the floor with Denny lying on top of Ames.

Both were dead.

"Get back inside!" Clint shouted at Bride, who obeyed without question and slammed the door.

Clint went over to the fallen gunmen, kicked their guns away, and then bent to check and make sure they were both dead.

Bridget stuck her head out the door, wrapped in a sheet.

"Get dressed," he told her. "We're going to have a lot of company."

TWENTY-SEVEN

Clint managed to get his trousers on before the sheriff arrived. By that time other guests had crowded their way into the hall.

"Everybody back into your rooms!" Cargill shouted. "Come on, get out of the hall so can find out what happened."

Slowly the people drifted back to their own rooms. Finally, there were only Clint and the sheriff standing in the hallway with the two bodies.

"Why doesn't this surprise me?" Cargill asked. "What happened?"

"Hey," Clint said, "I was minding my own business in my room when I heard a woman scream. I opened my door, and these fellas were there with guns in their hands. They turned their guns on me and I had no choice."

Cargill shook his head, then walked to the bodies to check them.

"You know them?" Clint asked.

"I know this one," the sheriff said, nudging a man with his toe. "His name's Denny Moore. Don't know this other one."

"There was a third," Clint said, "but he ran off."

The sheriff looked around.

"What's wrong?" Clint asked.

"If you worked in a hotel and there was a shootin'," Cargill asked, "what would you do?"

"I'd try and see what was happening."

"So where's the clerk?"

Clint shrugged.

"I'm gonna get some boys to remove these bodies," Cargill said, "and then I'm gonna find that clerk and see what he knows."

"Let me get dressed," Clint said, "and I'll join you."

"Yeah."

Clint went into his room. Bridget was seated on the bed, wearing her nightgown.

"Who were they?"

"I don't know."

"What did they want?"

"I don't know for sure, but I can guess," he said, pulling on his shirt. "Me."

"And Bride saw them," she said. "She must have awakened and was looking for me."

"If they were coming for me, she may have saved my—and your—life. But you'll have to deal with that," Clint said. "I'm going to join the sheriff and see what we can find out about these men. There was a third who ran away. Maybe we can find him."

"I'll think of something to tell her," she said. "You go on."

Clint pulled on his boots and stood up.

"I'll talk to you later," he said. "See if you can calm your sister down."

"I will."

He went out the door.

When Clint got to the lobby, the sheriff was standing at the front desk with the clerk. He'd had to step over the bodies of the two men in the hall, as the sheriff had not yet succeeded in having them removed.

"Got a few men comin' in to take those bodies out," he said to Clint.

Clint recognized the clerk as the one who had checked him in.

"This is Roscoe," the sheriff said. "We're havin' us a talk."

"I tol' ya," the clerk said. "I didn't see nothin'."

"You were crouched down behind the desk," the sheriff pointed out.

"That's why I didn't see nothin'."

"But why were you crouched down?" Cargill asked. "You must have seen somethin'."

The clerk bit his lower lip, then asked, "Are you sure they're dead?"

"Two of them are," Clint said. "One of them ran out."

"Right through here," the sheriff added. "You musta seen somethin' then."

"Look," the clerk said, "I didn't have no choice. They pointed their guns at me."

"Okay," the sheriff said, "now we're gettin' somewhere. What happened?"

"These three men came into the lobby, pointed their guns at me, and told me to get behind the desk. I'm lucky they didn't kill me."

"No, they just tried to kill one of your guests," Cargill said. "Why didn't you come and get me?"

"They tol' me to stay behind the desk!"

"But then they went upstairs. You could've ran out then."

"I—I was scared."

"No shame there," Clint said. "Having guns pointed at you would scare anybody."

"Yeah," Cargill said with a frown, "I guess." He looked at the clerk. "Did you know the men?"

"I knew two of 'em," the clerk said. "One was called Denny, and another Ames."

"And the third one?" Cargill asked.

"I didn't know him."

That didn't make the sheriff happy.

"But I seen him before."

"When?"

"Earlier today," the man said. "He came in and said there was somethin' outside I should see. I went out, and then he ran off."

"How long were you gone?" Cargill asked.

"Minutes."

The lawman looked at Clint.

"Enough time for somebody to run in, look at the register, and get your room number."

"Oh, geez," the clerk said, "I'm gonna get fired."

"Relax, Roscoe," Clint said, "you didn't do anything wrong."

"I hope my boss agrees with you," Roscoe said.

Several men entered then and the sheriff instructed them to go upstairs and collect the bodies.

As the men carried the bodies down the stairs and into the lobby, Cargill had them wait while Roscoe looked at the bodies.

"That one's Denny," he said, "but do you recognize the other one?"

"Yeah," Roscoe said, "that's Ames."

"Take 'em out," the sheriff told the men.

The clerk went back behind the desk.

Cargill looked at Clint.

"I'll ask around in the saloons, see where those boys did their drinkin'. Maybe somebody can give me the name of the third one."

"If you find him, let me know," Clint said. "I'd like to talk to him."

"You still leavin' first thing?" Cargill asked.

"I intend to."

"Okay," the lawman said, "if I hear anythin' before you leave, I'll let you know."

"Much obliged, Sheriff."

"Yeah . . ." Cargill said, and left.

Clint looked at the clerk, who turned away, and then the Gunsmith went back upstairs.

TWENTY-EIGHT

When Bridget reentered her room, Bride was sitting on her bed, just staring.

"You promised," she said.

Bridget had thought of one or two stories to tell that would explain her absence from the room, but decided to simply tell the truth.

"You have a man," she said. "You're getting married. Why shouldn't I find a man in America as well?"

"Clint Adams is not going to marry you," Bride said.

"Who says I want to get married?" Her sister looked at her sharply.

"So you just want to be a whore?"

"I am not a whore, Bride," Bridget said. "I never have been. You know that."

"Momma said you were wild," Bride said. "She said you were born wild."

"She was probably right," Bridget said. She walked to her own bed and sat down. "You saved our lives with your scream."

Bride looked away.

"I was frightened," she said.

"Nevertheless," she said, "you warned Clint."

Now Bride looked at her sister.

"Were they here for him?"

"Probably."

"Three men to kill one?" Bride asked. "That's not fair."

"I don't think everyone in this country acts fairly, Bride."

Bride put her face in her hands.

"This is a terrible place," she said.

Bridget moved from her bed to her sister's, put her hands on her shoulders.

"You're forgetting all the beef," she said.

Bride leaned into her sister. Her shoulders were moving, and for a moment Bridget thought she was crying, but then she dropped her hands from her face and she realized her sister was laughing.

There was a knock at the door at that moment. Bride stopped laughing and tensed up.

"It's probably Clint," Bridget said.

Bride nodded as her sister went to the door.

"Everybody okay?" Clint asked.

"Yes," Bridget said, "we're fine. What happened?"

"The sheriff's trying to find out who the third man was, but I think these men were just trying to become famous by killing me."

"In your sleep?"

"They probably thought that was the safest way to do it."

"Will this keep us from leaving in the morning?" Bridget asked.

"It shouldn't," Clint said. "The sheriff wants us to go, so we'll probably go."

"Good," she said. "We want to leave this town."

"So do I," he said. "Get some sleep. I'll knock on the door early in the morning."

"Will we have time for breakfast?" Bride asked.

"I guess she's okay if she's thinking about food," Clint said. "Yes, Bride, we'll have time for breakfast, and I'll pick those extra supplies we talked about before we leave."

Bride just nodded.

"Good night, ladies."

"Good night, Clint," Bridget said. They gave each other a long look that said they had unfinished business—or pleasure—and then she closed the door.

TWENTY-NINE

Clint woke up early. He hadn't slept very well. He was upset that he'd had to kill two more men, and also that he and Bridget had been interrupted.

He got washed and dressed, took up his carpetbag, and then went across the hall to knock. The door was opened immediately. Both girls were dressed, and apparently hadn't slept any better than he had.

"Ready to eat?" he asked.

"I am," Bride said. "I need a good meal before we go back to bacon and beans."

"And biscuits," Clint said. "Don't forget I'll make some biscuits, too. They're great soaked in the bacon grease."

"Oh God . . ." Bride said.

"Come along," Bridget said, putting her arm around her sister. "It won't be that bad."

The two girls followed Clint along the hall and down the stairs to the lobby.

While they were having breakfast in the hotel dining room, the sheriff came walking in. He spotted Clint and went over to their table.

"Adams," he said.

"Sheriff," Clint greeted him. "These are the ladies who are traveling with me—Bridget and Bride Shaughnessy. Ladies, Sheriff Cargill."

Clint's introduction was so formal, the sheriff took his hat off.

"Nice to meet you, ladies."

"What's going on, Sheriff?"

"I found the third man," Cargill said. "His name's Fred Doolin. He says he and his friends were just lookin' to make a name for themselves."

"An Irishman?" Bridget asked.

"I guess so, ma'am," Cargill said.

"He should be ashamed of himself," Bride said.

"What will you do with him?" Bridget asked.

"Well, nothin' much, ma'am."

"Nothing?" she asked. "But he tried to kill Clint."

"Ma'am, beggin' your pardon, but he ran off before the shootin' even started. I can't really charge him with anythin'."

"That's a shame," Bridget said.

"Yeah," the sheriff said. He put his hat back on, looked at Clint. "I just wanted to let you know."

"That's what I figured," Clint said, "but thanks."

"When are you headin' out?"

"Soon as we finish up here, I'm going to pick up a few supplies, and we'll be on our way."

"Good," Cargill said. "We don't need any more trouble in Saint Joe."

Bride surprised Clint by coming to his defense.

"What happened last night was not Clint's fault," she said.

"Beggin' your pardon, ma'am," the lawman said, "but that don't matter. Trouble just follows him around." He looked at Clint again. "Have yourself a good trip."

"Yeah," Clint said.

The lawman turned and left.

The two women stared across the table at Clint.

"So when someone tries to kill, you," Bridget said, "it's your fault?"

"That's pretty much the way it is," Clint said.

"And you accept that?" Bride asked.

"I don't have much of a choice," Clint said, "do I?"

When they were finished with breakfast, they all walked to the livery stable to collect the wagon, the team, and Eclipse. Owen Brown was there, but he looked like he'd had himself a rough night.

Clint drove the wagon over to the general store with Bride in the back and Bridget next to him.

"Stay here," he said. "I'll get the supplies and be right back."

"Okay," Bridget said.

Clint climbed down and went inside. He bought some flour, canned peaches, and more coffee. He came out, went behind the wagon and tossed the supplies in, then climbed up on the seat.

"Ready?" he asked the girls.

"We're ready," Bridget said, and Bride nodded.

Clint was glad to be driving out of Saint Joe. Once the news got out that the three men had tried to kill him, somebody else might get the same idea. As long as nobody followed them and tried for him on the trail, they'd be okay.

THIRTY

A few nights of biscuits and peaches did nothing to improve the trip for Bride, who became more and more morose as they got closer to Council Bluffs. It also seemed to bother her that Bridget and Clint seemed to be growing more comfortable with each other during the six-day trip.

On the afternoon of the sixth day, Council Bluffs appeared ahead of them.

"There it is," Clint said, "From there we head west, and then the trip will really become rough."

"Rougher than this?" Bride complained. "Bridget—"

"Relax, Bride," Bridget said. "It'll be fine."

Right before entering the city, Clint heard Bride pleading with Bridget to let them go the rest of the way by rail . . .

"This trip is for you, Bride," Bridget said. "You have a husband waiting for you at the other end."

"A husband I don't want," Bride said. "You can have him, Bridget. When he sees us, he'll want you anyway."

"Nonsense," Bridget said. "You're going to get married when we reach Shasta, and I'm going to see America along the way. That is what we agreed . . ."

Clint knew that the sisters were going to keep arguing

the same points over and over, so he rode on ahead a ways
until he could no longer hear what they were saying.

It had been a while since Clint had been in Council Bluffs.
Always known as the jumping-off point for the trip west,
Council Bluffs used to be more mud than anything else. Things
had changed, though. The town had grown, and there were
buildings he'd never seen before, including a brand-new
livery stable.

He stopped the wagon in front of the equally new Bluffs
Hotel and helped the girls down. He took a bag for each
from the back of the wagon and walked them into the lobby.

"Wait here," he said, leaving them each in a chair. He went
to the desk to get rooms for them all—again, one room for
the sisters and one for him.

"How long will you be stayin', sir?" the desk clerk asked.

"One night."

"Yes, sir."

Clint signed the register and the clerk gave him the keys.

"Thank you."

"Do the ladies need help getting upstairs, sir?" the clerk
asked. He was a young man, and he was giving Bridget and
Bride some approving glances.

"No, that won't be necessary," Clint said.

He went over to the girls and said, "Come on. I'll walk
you to your room."

They stood up and preceded him up the stairs.

After Clint got the two tired girls installed in their room,
he went back down to the lobby.

"Hey, mister," the clerk said, "looks like somebody's
interested in your wagon."

"Thanks," Clint said.

He went outside, saw that two men were peering into the
rear of the wagon. One of them came out with a bag that
belonged to one of the girls.

"This bag sure smells nice, Ben," he said to his friend.

Ben leaned in, sniffed, and said, "It sure does, Zack. Wonder what's in it?"

"You won't find out today, boys," Clint said. "Put it back."

The two men turned and looked at Clint. They were wearing worn trousers and skins that looked like bearskins. In any case, they smelled like bears. There was so much grime on their faces he couldn't tell how old they were. One wore a gun in a worn leather holster; the other had a bandolier across his chest and a rifle in his hand.

"This wagon yours?" the man with the pistol asked. He was holding the bag. So he was Zack, Clint figured.

"It is."

Zack held the bag to his nose.

"Sure does smell good. You like smellin' good, mister?"

"I'd rather smell good than smell like a couple of bears," Clint said.

"You sayin' me and my brother smell like bears?" Zack demanded.

"I'm saying you stink like a couple of bears," Clint said. "Now put the bag back."

Ben started to lift his rifle.

"If your brother brings that rifle up any higher, I'll kill him," Clint said.

Zack studied Clint, then lifted a hand to stay his brother's actions.

"Now put the bag back in the wagon."

Zack tossed the bag back.

"Now walk away, both of you," Clint said.

"You talk big, mister," Zack said.

"I'll do more than talk if you don't walk away."

Zack studied Clint a little longer.

"Lemme kill 'im, Zack," Ben said.

"Naw, naw," Zack said. "Look at him, Ben. He's a gunny. He wants you to try to kill him, so he can kill you."

"But—"

"We ain't gunmen, gunny," Zack said to Clint. "We'll see you another time."

"I'll look forward to it," Clint said.

"Come on, Ben."

"But Zack—"

"Do as I say!" Zack snapped.

He walked away. Ben gave Clint a long look, and for a moment Clint thought he was going to go against his brother's words, but in the end, he turned and followed after him.

THIRTY-ONE

Clint took the wagon and Eclipse to the livery stable, arranged with the liveryman to have them ready early the next morning.

"Not stayin' real long?" the man asked.

"Just heading west," Clint said.

"Some folks actually come here and stay a few days now," the man said. "We got everything—saloons, girls, gamblin'—"

"Men who smell like bears," Clint said.

"Ah," the man said, "you met Ben and Zack, the Lane brothers."

"What's their story?"

"Bad men who do bad things when they can get away with it. You got women with you?"

"I do."

"I'd keep an eye on them," the man said. "The Lane boys would rape 'em just as soon as look at 'em."

"What does the law say about that?"

"Well," the man said, "like I said, we got a lot of things we never used to have. We got saloons, girls, gamblin' . . . but we ain't got a lawman."

"Why not?"

"Well, we had one up to about a week ago."

"And what happened?"

"The Lane boys killed 'im."

It soon became clear that the Lane boys had shown up a few weeks before, and had been running roughshod over the town ever since. And there was nobody who could stop them. Not yet anyway.

Clint went directly back to the hotel to talk to the girls.

"So we have to stay inside the whole time we're here?" Bride asked.

"We're only going to be here overnight," Clint said.

"You say these men killed the local sheriff?" Bridget cried.

"They did."

"And no one in town can stop them?"

"Apparently not."

"Well then, you must stop them."

"Me? Why?"

"Because you can," Bridget said.

"I didn't come here to bring law and order to Council Bluffs," Clint said. "I'm here to take you ladies west. That's my task."

"But you killed those men in Saint Joseph," Bridget pointed out.

"Those men were going to try to kill me," Clint explained.

"Perhaps these men will try also," Bride said.

"Not if we leave town first."

"You're not afraid of these men, are you?" Bride asked.

"I'm only afraid I might suffocate if I have to get near them again."

"We have to eat," Bridget said.

"I expected that comment to come from Bride."

"We have to eat," Bride agreed.

"I saw a café across the street," he said. "We'll walk over there, eat, and then come back and stay in."

"Well," Bride said, "you're in charge."

"That's right," Clint said. "I am. Ready to go eat?"

They went down through the lobby, under the watchful eye of the clerk, walked outside, and crossed the street. The café was small, had been built recently. Inside there were about ten tables. Only two of them were in use at that moment.

A waiter came and asked, "Three of you?"

"That's right."

"This way."

He started off and Clint said, "No, that one." He pointed to a table in the back.

"Okay."

They walked to the table and sat down.

"What can get you?" the waiter asked.

"Steaks all around. Coffee for me, tea for the ladies."

"No," Bride said, "I will have coffee."

"So will I," Bridget said.

"You heard the ladies," Clint said. "Coffee all around, too."

"Yes, sir. Comin' up."

Clint kept his eyes on the door, and the windows. He didn't see the Lane brothers on the street, but that didn't mean they wouldn't show up.

The hotel clerk looked up as two men came in from the back, having used the rear door to enter. Actually, he smelled them before he saw them.

"Who's the good-smellin' man, Leo?" Zack asked.

Leo tried to answer and not breathe at the same time.

"His name's Clint Adams, Zack."

"Yer lyin'," Ben said.

"I ain't," Leo said. "He wrote it right here in the register."

"Then he's lyin'," Ben said. "Ain't he, Zack?"

"I don't think so, Ben," Zack said. "Not the way he stood there talkin' to us."

"Then if he's the Gunsmith . . ."

"He would've killed you easy," Zack said. "Without a thought."

"Jesus . . ."

"How long is he stayin'?" Zack asked Leo.

"Only 'til mornin'."

"And who's he got with him?"

Leo smiled.

"Two of the prettiest gals you'd ever wanna see," he said.

"That a fact?" Ben asked.

"That's a fact," Leo said. "And they smell real nice, too."

Zack and Ben exchanged a glance, and then Zack said to Leo, "Okay, little brother. Thanks."

"Sure, Zack."

Zack and Ben returned to the rear of the hotel, stepped out the back door, and stopped short.

"What the—" Zack said.

There were five men standing there, all armed.

"Take it easy," Troy Ahern said, "we just want to talk."

"About what?"

"About a subject we're all interested in," Ahern said. "The Gunsmith and his two ladies."

Zack and Ben exchanged a glance.

"We're also buyin' the drinks," Ahern added.

"Well, okay, then," Zack said. "We're willin' ta listen."

"What's a good place to drink?" Ahern asked him.

"My brother and me got just the place," Zack said. "Follow us."

THIRTY-TWO

"You look worried," Bride said while they ate.

"I am."

"About getting killed?"

"I'm worried about the two of you," Clint said. "If something happens to me, how will you get to Shasta?"

"Nothing will happen to you," Bridget said.

"Well, we had a close call in Saint Joe," he said. "We still don't know if somebody's following us from New York, and now we have to worry about these two jaspers who smell like bears."

"Well then," Bride said, "maybe you should tell us how to get there from here, just in case something does happen."

"Bride!"

"No, she's right," Clint said. "You girls should know how to get to Shasta on your own, just in case."

"Well . . . all right," Bridget said.

"Let's go back to the hotel so we can talk about it."

"Let's have some pie first," Bride suggested.

It was the last building in Council Bluffs—or the first, depending on which end of town you entered from. It also looked like the oldest building in town. It was one story, only because the second story had long since fallen in on itself.

"You sure this place will stand up?" Ahern asked.

"It'll stand," Zack said. "We come here all the time. Come on."

Ahern, Phil Kemper, and the three other men they had hired followed the Lane brothers into the saloon, which had no name on it.

Inside there were several tables, one of which had a leg missing and was jammed against the wall, and some rickety chairs. The handful of customers didn't look up as the seven men entered.

The bartender watched the Lane boys lead the other five men to the bar and asked, "Who're yer new friends, Zack?"

"Set us up with some drinks, Andy," Zack said, "and maybe we'll all find out."

"You got it."

"Beer for us," Ahern said.

"Well then," Zack said, "beer for everybody, on my new friend."

As they walked through the lobby of the hotel, Clint sniffed the air carefully.

"Did you smell that?" he asked the girls when they got to his room.

"Smell what?" Bride asked.

"Down in the lobby."

"It did smell rather rank," Bridget said.

"That's what those two men smelled like," he said. "They were in the hotel."

"Maybe," she said, "it's like what happened in Saint Joe. They looked at the register to see who you are. And now that they do, they'll go away."

"I doubt it," he said. "That's not how men react when they find out who I am."

"I don't understand," Bridget said. "Do they want to die?"

"They all think they'll be the one," Clint said.

"The one?" Bride asked.

"The one who kills me," Clint said.

"I don't understand why Western men think killing is so important," Bride said.

"It's like that everywhere, Bride," Bridget said, "not only here in America."

"Okay," Clint said, "let's talk about getting to Shasta County . . ."

"So let me get this straight," Zack said. "You wanna pay us to not only kill the Gunsmith, but those two women with him?"

"No," Ahern said. "We want you to kill the women. We don't care what you do with Clint Adams."

"And what will you be doin'?" Ben asked.

"My friend Kemper there and me will be payin' you," Ahern said.

"And these other fellers?" Zack asked.

"They're yours, if you want them," Ahern said. "We're payin' them, too."

Zack looked at his brother, who always left the business decisions up to his brother.

"Well?" Ahern asked.

"I guess," Zack said, "this is all gonna depend on how much you're payin' us."

"Then let's get some more drinks and talk about that," Ahern said.

After Clint explained to the girls the route from Council Bluffs to Shasta County, he went back down to the lobby. He could still smell the two men there. He walked to the door and looked out, then turned and looked at the desk clerk.

"You smell that?" Clint asked.

"Smell what, sir?" the clerk asked.

Clint crossed the lobby to stand right in front of the desk.

"Smells like wet bear," Clint said. "Dirty wet bear. You don't smell it?"

The clerk made a show of sniffing the air, then said, "Sir, I don't—"

"Don't bother lying," Clint said. "I can smell those two from here."

The clerk fell silent.

"What did they want?" Clint asked.

"Um, they just wanted to know who you are."

"Did you tell them?"

"I did."

"Why?"

"I figured if they knew, they'd leave you alone, and you wouldn't have to kill them."

"Why'd you warn me that they were going through my wagon?"

The clerk shrugged.

"Seemed like the right thing to do."

Clint reached out and grabbed the young man's wrist.

"I'm going to need a better reason than that."

"Okay, okay," the clerk said. Clint released him. "I was hopin' you'd kill 'em."

"Why?"

The clerk hesitated, then said, "They're my brothers."

"And you want me to kill them?"

"I came here to get away from them," the clerk said. "They found me, and ever since they been here, they've been—well, they killed the sheriff. That ought to tell you the kind of men they are."

"And you want them dead?"

"I'd like them to leave town," the young man said, "but if that can't happen, yeah. I want them dead. I want them out of my life. There's something wrong with them."

"Okay," Clint said, "say I believe you. What will they do next?"

"They're gonna try to figure out a way to kill you, and to have your women."

"Will they come during the night?"

"Maybe."

"Okay," Clint said, "I want two new rooms, but I don't want you to change the room numbers on the register."

"O-Okay."

Clint collected the two new keys.

"If you tell them what room I'm in," Clint said, "or the ladies are in, I'll come for you when I'm done with them. Do you understand?"

"Y-Yessir," the clerk said. "I understand."

"What's your name?"

"Leo."

"Okay, Leo," Clint said. "I don't want to kill your brothers, but with no law in town, if they come for me, I will."

Clint went upstairs to move the girls and himself to new rooms.

Leo breathed a sigh of relief. He hadn't wanted the Gunsmith to know he was brother to Zack and Ben, but his plan might still work. And if he did manage to get Adams to kill his brothers, the whole town would owe him a debt of gratitude.

THIRTY-THREE

It wasn't dark yet.

Bridget and Bride moved into their new room, and Bridget lay down on her bed to rest. Before long she was breathing evenly and deeply asleep.

Bride walked to the window and looked out. The street was busy. Council Bluffs was not the kind of town Saint Joe had been. And it certainly wasn't what Saint Louis had been. Both of those were places she wished she'd had a chance to look at.

It seemed to her that everybody was getting to do what they wanted to do but her. She was just supposed to travel to Shasta County and marry a man forty years older than she was. If she was going to do that, she'd like to have a good time somewhere along the way first.

She looked at Bridget again. She was still fast asleep. And she was pretty sure Clint was in his room.

She went to the door, listened to see if anyone was in the hall, then opened it and slipped out.

Bridget came awake slowly. She was surprised she had fallen asleep, and now she was groggy as she woke.

"Wow," she said, "I really fell asleep. Bride?"

She turned in her bed, expecting to see her sister in the other. There was only one place she could think her sister might have gone.

She got up, went across the hall, and knocked on Clint's door. It never occurred to her that her sister and Clint might be doing what she and Clint had been doing when they were interrupted in Saint Joseph. She simply could not think of anyplace else Bride could be.

Clint opened the door, smiled when he saw Bridget.

"Is Bride here?" Bridget asked immediately.

"No, she's not."

"Have you seen her in the past hour or so?"

"No."

"She's gone, Clint," she said. "I don't know where she is."

"Wait," he said. He got his gun from the bedpost, strapped it on, and put on his hat.

"Wait in your room," he said. "I'll find her."

"I want to come—"

"I can't be worried about both of you," he said. "Just wait and I'll find her. I promise."

"Please do."

He closed his door and went down to the lobby.

Kemper couldn't believe his eyes when the girl came out of the hotel.

"Jesus," he said to himself.

He had two choices: Kill her now, or find Ahern and tell him. She began to walk down the street at a leisurely pace, apparently just sightseeing as dusk fell.

He decided to go tell Ahern and let him decide what to do.

Clint came down to the lobby and approached the desk. The clerk looked at him with obvious concern, if not fear.

"Have you seen one of the girls in the past hour?"

"Yeah," he said, "I saw one of 'em come down a little

while ago and go out. I don't know which one it was. They look alike."

"Where'd she go?"

"Out," Leo said. "I don't know where."

"Why didn't you stop her?"

The clerk just shrugged.

Clint went outside, stopped, and looked both ways. He also looked across the street to see if anyone was watching the hotel. Finally, he had to pick a direction, so he went to the right.

Ahern turned the whore over onto her belly, then lifted her butt into the air while her face was buried in the pillow. She had a big, pale ass, and seeing it hiked up in the air like that increased his level of excitement.

He pushed his raging cock up between her thighs and into her wet pussy. She gasped, then made the appropriate noises as he began driving himself in and out of her. He gripped her hips and gritted his teeth each time he slammed into her. The room filled with the sound of slapping flesh—and then there was a knock on the door.

"What, damnit?" Ahern shouted.

There was some hesitation, and then Kemper's voice said, "I got somethin' important to tell you."

Ahern withdrew from the whore's cunt, his penis wet and pulsing.

"It better be important," he growled on his way to the door.

The whore turned over onto her back, her plain face looking bored. Her only concern was that she had already been paid, so she didn't care what happened after that.

Ahern yanked the door open and said, "What?"

Kemper ignored his partner's nudity and said, "You're not gonna believe this."

THIRTY-FOUR

If Bride was simply wandering the streets, Clint's goal was to find her before anyone else did—the brothers, or someone following them from New York. She'd obviously left the room under her own power. Nobody could have taken her without waking Bridget, and why take one and leave the other? So she was out having a look around Council Bluffs on her own, but she was putting all their lives in jeopardy.

Where the hell was she?

Since Kemper knew the direction the girl had gone, he and Ahern—and the Lane Brothers—had the advantage over Clint.

Ahern left the other three men behind, figuring they didn't need all of them to simply grab the girl off the street. The fragrant Lane Brothers could take care of that themselves.

"Is that her?" Zack asked.

He pointed across the street. They all saw a red-haired woman in a green shirt and a pair of brown britches walking down the street like she didn't have any idea where she was.

"That's her," Ahern said. "Get her."

"Now?" Ben asked. "On the street?"

"I don't mean kill her," Ahern said. "I mean grab her."

"And do what?" Zack asked.

Ahern looked around, then pointed.

"Bring her into that saloon."

"There's people in that saloon," Ben said.

"I'll take care of it," Ahern said. "Go!"

The Lane brothers started across the street toward the girl. Ahern and Kemper went into the saloon. There was a bored bartender and three patrons, one at the bar and two at tables.

Ahern approached the bartender and asked, "How good are you at minding your own business?"

"I'm real good at it."

"And these fellas?"

"They wouldn't even notice if the place was on fire," the bartender said.

"You sure?"

"Mister," the barman said, "go ahead and fire a shot and see what happens."

"I'm gonna take your word for it," Ahern said. "If you're wrong, it's gonna be too bad."

"Don't worry," the bartender said. "I seen a lot of things."

Ahern turned to Kemper and said, "Watch the door."

Outside, the brothers reached the girl, one on either side of her.

Bride stopped and looked at the two of them.

"What do you want?" she demanded.

"You," Zack said. He took one arm, and Ben took the other.

"She sure is pretty, Zack."

"Yeah, she is," Zack said.

Suddenly, Bride realized who they were, mainly because of the smell.

"You're making a mistake," she said.

"Are we?"

"Mr. Adams won't like this."

"Adams?"

"He's the Gunsmith," she said. "I'm with him."

"You was with him, girlie," Zack said. "Now you're with us."

They tightened their holds on her arms and dragged her into the street.

"Here they come," Kemper said.

"Good," Ahern said, "when they come in, you go and get the other boys."

"But I thought—"

"I changed my mind," Ahern said. "We're gonna use this girl to have Adams bring us the other one. Then we'll have to kill them all. We're gonna need those boys."

"Okay," Kemper said.

The Lanes came through the batwing doors, dragging the girl between them.

"We got 'er," Zack said.

"She's pretty," Ben said.

"You have to let me go!" Bride said. "Are you in charge here?"

Ahern said, "I am."

"Tell these men to let me go. Or you'll have to deal with the Gunsmith."

"Lady," Ahern said, "I'm countin' on it."

THIRTY-FIVE

When the rest of the men arrived, Ahern said to one named Toland, "Go and find the Gunsmith."

"What?"

"He's probably out lookin' for this girl," Ahern said. "Tell him where we are, and that we have her and want the other one. Now, this is important."

"What is?"

"Don't tell him about me or Kemper. As far as he's concerned, it's you three, and those two."

"And why do I tell him we have the girl and want the other one?"

"Don't tell him why," Ahern said. "Just tell him you do."

"H-He might kill me."

"He won't lay a finger on you," Ahern said. "Not while we have her."

"Can I—can I take one of the others?"

"Sure," Ahern said, "take somebody with you. But go!"

"Jennings, come on."

"Me?"

"Go!" Ahern said.

They went.

* * *

Obviously, he had gone the wrong way.

Clint walked to the end of Council Bluffs, where there was a falling-down saloon, and did not see Bride. She must have gone the other way. He quickly retraced his steps, and as he approached his hotel, he saw two men walking toward him.

He stopped to see what they'd do . . . and they stopped.

"You boys looking for me?" he asked.

"You Adams?" one asked.

"I am."

"We got your girl," he said.

"And we want the other one."

"What keeps me from killing you right now?" Clint asked.

Both men seemed startled by the question.

"Uh, like I said, we got your girl," one of them said. "If you kill us, our friends will kill her."

"And if I bring you the other girl, you'll kill both . . . and probably me. Looks like a Mexican standoff to me."

The two men obviously did not know what to do with that.

"Okay," Clint said, "you fellas aren't in charge, so go back and tell your boss what I said. I'll be at my hotel."

The two men exchanged an anxious glance.

"Go!" Clint said. "I'm not going to shoot you in the back."

They turned and ran.

Clint went back to the hotel, knocked on Bridget's door. She opened it with a worried look on her face.

"Where is she?"

"Take it easy."

"Is she all right?"

"She's fine," Clint said, "but they have her."

"Who has her?"

"I'm not sure," Clint said, "but somebody does. I talked to two of them, but they're not in charge."

"Then who is?"

"That's what I'm trying to find out."

"I have to go—" she said, bolting into the hall. He grabbed her and stopped her.

"Bridget, you don't even know where you're going," he said.

"I have to do something!"

"You have to do the same thing I'm going to do."

"What's that?"

"Wait."

THIRTY-SIX

"What happened?" Ahern asked as the two men entered the small saloon.

"He said we had a Mexican standoff," Jennings said.

"How did he figure that?"

"Well, we got one girl, he's got the other one," Toland said.

"That ain't no Mexican standoff," Ahern said. "Where is he?"

"At his hotel, with the other girl."

"Zack, you and your brother go get him. Bring him back here."

"Okay," Zack said. "Okay if we bring him back dead?"

"I don't care," Ahern said, "but I want that girl. I want to kill them together."

As the Lane brothers left, Bride looked at Ahern as if he was crazy.

"Why are you doing this?" she asked.

"If I told you, little girl," Ahern said, "you probably wouldn't believe me."

"Here they come," Clint said, looking out his window. "Stay here."

"I want to come," Bridget said. "She's my sister!"

"Bridget," Clint said, "it's obvious they want both of you. I don't want the two of you in the same place at the same time."

"But—"

"Stay here!"

He left the room, hoping she'd obey him, but doubting it.

He made it to the lobby as the Lane boys entered. Leo was wide-eyed at the desk, hoping he was about to see what he wanted to see.

"Adams!" Zack shouted. "Yer comin' with us."

And what makes you think that?" Clint asked.

"We got your girl."

"You've got one of my girls," Clint said. "Actually, I like the one I got better. You can have the other one. She's a pain in the neck."

"Wha—" Ben said.

"That ain't the way it's gonna happen," Zack said. "Yer comin'—"

Clint thought he had the situation under control until he heard a voice from the stairway.

"Where's my sister?"

He closed his eyes and shook his head. The situation had just changed . . .

Ahern walked over to Bride and took her chin in his hand.

"You are kinda good-looking," he said. "I think all the men in this place would like a turn with you."

"A turn?"

"Using you," Ahern said. "Having you. You know what I mean?" He put his face close to hers. "Rape!"

She caught her breath. When he released her chin, she looked around the room, as if seeking someone who would help her. Instead she found herself facing hungry looks— from everyone.

"Hey, are we included?" one of the patrons asked.

"Sure, why not?" Ahern asked. "You're here, right?"

Bride felt tears come to her eyes.

"Go upstairs, Bridget," Clint said.

"Stay there, girlie!" Zack said. "If ya wanna see yer sister alive."

"Where is she?"

"She's havin' herself a time in a saloon," Zack said. "You're gonna have yerself a time, too."

"You animal!" Bridget shouted.

"Now that ain't nice talk," Zack said.

"If I had a gun, I would kill you now," Bridget said.

"Zack," Ben said, "I should kill her now myself." He started to raise his rifle.

"Ben—" Zack said.

Clint didn't wait to see if Ben was going to heed his brother's warning. He drew and fired. Ben staggered, dropped his rifle, said, "Zack," and fell to the floor.

"Goddamnit!" Zack said.

"Clint!" Bridget shouted.

He turned in time to see Leo come out from beneath the desk with a gun. For a moment he thought the younger man was going to shoot his own brother, but then he brought the gun to bear on Clint. He had no choice. He fired, knocking the clerk back against the wall, and then down.

He turned back in time to see Zack pulling his gun, and fired again.

A few streets away, in the saloon, Ahern heard the shots. Kemper was looking out the door.

"Whataya see?" Ahern asked.

"Nothin'," Kemper said.

Ahern looked at the other three men.

"They got 'im," Jennings said. "They musta."

"No!" Bride said.

"Don't worry," Ahern said to her, "your sister will be joinin' you shortly."

Bride put her head down on the table and started to cry. If only she'd stayed in her room. If only . . .

THIRTY-SEVEN

Clint checked all the bodies to be sure they were dead, then lingered standing over Leo, the young clerk.

"This boy lied to me," he said.

Bridget joined him, looked down at Leo, then looked away.

"He told me he wanted me to kill his brothers," Clint said, "when all along he was working with them."

"What about Bride?" Bridget asked.

"We know she's in a saloon," he said. "We just have to figure out which one."

"How do we do that?"

"Well," Clint said, stepping out from behind the desk, "it won't be a busy saloon."

"Why not?"

"Too many people in the way," Clint explained, "and too much of a chance somebody would get brave and try to intervene when they saw a woman in trouble."

"What does that leave?"

"Small saloons. There's probably a few."

"Who can we ask?"

"Nobody," Clint said. "We'll have to go and look."

"Both of us?"

"Yes," Clint said. "I can't leave you here."

"Then when do we go?"

"Now," Clint said. "Can you shoot?"

"I never have."

Clint leaned over and picked up the clerk's gun, a .32 Colt. Small enough for someone who had never fired a gun before.

"Take this," he said, handing it to her.

"What do I do?"

"You point and shoot," Clint said, "but right now just tuck it into your belt. Don't take it out unless I start shooting. If that happens, then you start shooting."

"At what?"

"At anything," Clint said. "Just close your eyes and keep pulling the trigger until the gun is empty."

"What will that do?"

"It'll be a distraction," Clint said. "Come on, we're going out the back."

"What about these bodies?"

"Don't worry about them," Clint said. "There are probably going to be a lot more before we're done."

Ahern walked over to stand next to Kemper and look out at the street. It was dark now, and a couple of men were walking around lighting streetlamps.

"No sign of them?" he asked.

"None."

"Those idiots!" Ahern swore.

"They got themselves killed."

"Looks like it."

Ahern looked over at Bride, who was surrounded by the other three men. Jennings was touching her and she was cringing from him.

"Adams is probably on his way here, but he ain't comin' in the front door."

"So what do we do?" Kemper asked.

"We get ready for him," Ahern said. "We have the girl, so he has to come to us. He's not gonna draw us out into the street."

Ahern turned and said, "Jennings, get on the back door."

"Right." He pulled himself away from Bride and went to the back of the room.

"Bartender!"

"Yeah?" the bored man asked.

"Is there any way to get in here from above?"

"There used to be a second floor, but it collapsed a long time ago."

Ahern took that to mean no.

"You other two, keep an eye on the windows. Kemper, you stay on the door."

"What are you gonna do?" Kemper asked.

"I'm gonna sit with the young lady," Ahern said. "If anything goes wrong, I'm gonna put a bullet in her brain first thing."

He went over and sat at the table with Bride.

"Everybody set?" he asked.

They all nodded.

Clint and Bridget left by the back door of the hotel and made their way to the street.

"We have to stay in the shadows until we find out what saloon they're in."

"All right."

"We'll work one side of the street, and then the other. Stay behind me, Bridget. No matter what you see, stay with me. If anything goes wrong, it could cost Bride her life. Do you understand?"

"I understand." He noticed she had her hand on the gun in her belt.

"And keep your hand off the gun," he said, wondering if it was a bad idea to give it to her. "You're liable to shoot yourself."

She snatched her hand away from the gun.

THIRTY-EIGHT

"There," Clint said. He pointed across the street.

"Are you sure?"

"Yes."

"How?"

"It's small, it's not busy," Clint said. "Nobody has gone in or out while we're been watching. And there's a man standing in the door."

"I don't see him."

"I do," Clint said. "He's trying not to be seen, but I see him."

"So what do we do now?"

"We come up with a plan."

"You don't have a plan already?"

"There's no way to form a plan until you know what you're dealing with," Clint said. "We don't know how many men with guns there are inside."

"How do we find out?"

Clint wished he'd kept one of the brothers alive for that information.

"I'm going to have to get a look inside that saloon."

Exasperated, Bridget asked, "How are you going to do that?"

"I'm going to have to do what's unexpected," he said. "I have to walk in there."

"Ahern!" Kemper called.

"What?"

"Remember what you said about Adams not comin' in the front door?"

"Yeah, why?"

Kemper pointed and said, "Here he comes."

Ahern got up and rushed to the door. Sure enough, Clint Adams was crossing the street, heading for the front door.

"What's he tryin' to do?" Kemper asked.

"He's tryin' to get the better of us," Ahern said. "Do the unexpected."

"So what do we do?"

"I'm gonna go back to my table," Ahern said, "and stay to my plan."

"And what do I do?"

Ahern slapped Kemper on the shoulder and said, "You let him in."

Clint approached the batwing doors of the saloon. The man standing there backed away a few steps to let him enter, which he did.

He stood just inside the door and did a quick count. Nine men, but that included the bartender, so that left eight. Three other men had all the appearance of people who had been drinking all day. By Clint's count, he had five men to worry about.

One of them was sitting with Bride, whose face was tearstained. She stared at Clint with pleading eyes.

"Hi, Bride."

"Clint—" she started, but the man sitting with her cut her off by grabbing her arm.

"Adams, my name is Ahern," he said. "Where's the other sister?"

"Where you can't get to her."

"Well, that's not a good idea," Ahern said. "But I've got this one, and I've got you. Two out of three ain't bad. That puts me in control."

"Really?" Clint asked. "You really think you've got control in this situation?"

It got very quiet in the room.

"Let me tell you what happens if anybody goes for a gun," Clint said. "I kill you first. No matter what happens, you die."

Everybody started exchanging glances.

"How's that for being in control?" Clint asked.

THIRTY-NINE

The room remained quiet for several long seconds. The bartender shifted uncomfortably.

"Keep your hands on the bar, barkeep," Clint said.

"Hey," the bartender said, putting his hands up, "I ain't with them."

Clint was sure that was right, but he'd had a hotel desk clerk tell him the same thing.

"Where are the Lane brothers?" Ahern asked.

"They're dead," Clint said, "on the floor of the hotel lobby, along with their brother."

"Brother?"

"The desk clerk."

"I don't know what you're talkin' about."

"It's not important," Clint said. "I think it's time for me to leave with Bride."

"I don't think so," Ahern said. He tightened his grip on her arm, to the point where she winced in pain. "I kinda like havin' her here."

"This could get messy," Clint said.

"I'll tell you how to keep it from gettin' messy," Ahern said. "Bring me the other sister, and then you can walk away."

"Really?" Clint said. "Can I think about that?"

"No," Ahern said. "I want you to bring me the other girl in fifteen minutes, or I'll put a bullet in this sister's brain."

Bride made a high-pitched noise.

"Don't worry, Bride," Clint said. "Everything's going to be all right."

"Is it?" Ahern asked.

"Let's all hope so," Clint said. "So, fifteen minutes, huh?"

"Fifteen."

Clint backed out the doors.

"I'll be back."

He backed up all the way to the street, then turned and walked across.

Kemper looked at Ahern and asked, "What do you think?"

"He's gonna try somethin'," Ahern said, "but there are five of us, and we're ready."

Ahern looked around at the other men and repeated, "We're ready, right?"

They nodded, though not enthusiastically.

Clint worked his way through the shadows to the alley where he had left Bridget.

"Bridget!"

"Here," she said.

He moved into the alley and founded her crouched down. He reached down, took her by the arms, and lifted her to her feet.

"Hold on to me," she said. "My legs are weak."

He held her in his arms and said, "Bride's fine. There are nine men in that saloon—"

"Nine?"

"But we only have to worry about five of them."

"Five doesn't sound much better."

"We have about fourteen minutes," Clint said. "Come on."

"Where?"

"We have to go back to the hotel," Clint said. "There's something there I need."

"What?"

"More guns!"

FORTY

For a moment he considered Ben's rifle, but there was no way he could walk into that saloon carrying a rifle. That would make it obvious that he wasn't there to turn the girls over and walk away.

"Do you really believe he would let you walk away?" Bridget asked.

"Not at all," Clint said. "He's going to try to kill me—all of us."

"What are we going to do?"

"We're not going to let him."

Clint walked to the fallen Zack and picked up his gun.

It was an ancient Navy Colt, fully loaded, and clean enough to still work.

He wanted to go up to his room and get his Colt New Line, but time was running out.

"All right," he said, "we've got to get back."

"But what's the plan?" she asked.

"You wait for me to start shooting," he said, "and then you do the same."

"That's it?"

"That's it."

"I'm not going to be any help, Clint," she said. "You have to face five men alone. They'll kill you."

"I'm hoping that your shooting will confuse them enough to give me an edge," Clint said.

"Okay."

They left the hotel and headed back to the saloon.

Clint stopped across the street from the saloon, still in the shadows.

"Give me your gun," he said.

"Why?"

"Just do it."

She took it from the front of her belt and handed it to him. He turned her around and stuck it in the back of her belt. He had the Navy Colt in the same place in his belt.

"Okay," Clint said, "before we go in, there's something else I should have told you."

"What's that?"

"When the shooting starts," Clint said, "you hit the floor, and keep pulling your trigger." He started to step into the street.

"Wait," she said.

He stopped and looked at her.

"What?"

"What if I shoot you by accident?"

"Just don't."

They started across the street.

"Ahern!"

"Yeah?"

Kemper pointed and said, "Here they come."

"The girl, too?"

"Yep."

"Okay," Ahern said, looking around. "As soon as they walk in, kill Adams. After that we'll take care of the girls."

Bride was sitting still, just staring straight ahead. She hadn't made a sound or shed a tear since Clint had left.

"Buck up, sweetheart," Ahern said, putting his hand on the back of her neck, "you're about to have a family reunion."

FORTY-ONE

Clint stepped up onto the boardwalk, Bridget right next to him. He was wondering if he could have thought of a way to do this without her, given a little more time. But there was no time.

"Ready?" he asked.

"Let's go get my sister," she said.

They went through the batwing doors.

"Get down!" Bride shouted before anybody had a chance to pull their gun.

The shout galvanized everyone into action.

Clint drew his gun, slapped Kemper in the face with it, since he was standing so close. The man went down hard.

Jennings, Toland, and the other man all drew their weapons.

Ahern took his hand from Bride's neck, but before he could do anything, she grabbed it and bit it.

Bridget hit the floor, pulled the gun from the back of her pants, and started pulling the trigger with her eyes closed, hoping she wouldn't hit Clint or Bride.

Clint was firing with his right hand even as he pulled the Navy Colt out with his left. In a split second he was firing with both hands. The Navy Colt was a single-action, so he had to pull back on the hammer with his thumb before each shot. It didn't slow him down much, though.

He killed Jennings, Toland, and the third man with three shots. He looked over at the man at the table, who was trying to shake Bride from his hand, but having a hard time of it.

Bridget ran out of bullets, kept pulling the trigger. The only sound in the room was the hammer falling on the empty chambers.

Ahern finally shook Bride off his hand, knocking her to the floor. She took a chunk of flesh with her. He then went for his gun.

"Don't!" Clint shouted.

"Go to hell!" Ahern shouted, dragging his gun from his holster with his injured hand.

Clint fired once. Ahern went over backward with his chair.

"Is it over?" Bridget asked from the floor.

"It's over."

Bridget and Bride both got off the floor and ran into each other's arms.

The patrons and bartender all got off the floor, where they'd dropped as soon as Bride had shouted.

Clint checked the bodies to make sure they were dead. Then he checked the man he had hit—Kemper—and was surprised to find two bullets in his chest. He wondered about that until he realized from the position the body was in, and where Bridget had been lying on the floor when she was shooting, that it had to be she who had shot and killed him.

He wasn't sure whether he was going to tell her that or not.

The bartender came over to him and said, "These fellers were sayin' you probably killed the Lane brothers. Is that true?"

"It's true."

"Well then, friend," the barman said, "you just did Council Bluffs a service."

Clint looked at the man and said, "It wasn't my intention. Council Bluffs should have found itself a new sheriff to do the job."

He walked over, collected the two Irish girls, and walked them out of the saloon.

FORTY-TWO

MORE THAN TWO MONTHS LATER

Bride was a lot more cooperative and less morose for the rest of the trip to Shasta, even though it was a bit harder. But at least nobody was trying to kill them.

They stopped at some towns along the way, but only to replenish supplies. They all agreed that staying in a hotel, even overnight, was inviting trouble. Somebody could see Clint, recognize him, and make a try for him, or someone could see the girls and become interested. Bridget and Bride had seen enough American men who were less than gentlemen. They didn't want to deal with any more.

So for the remainder of the trip they only had to deal with a broken wheel, an injured horse, the weather, a wolf who got too close to camp, and some renegades from a reservation who only wanted to trade.

Bridget did contract a fever while they were traveling through Colorado, but Bride nursed her back to health and they only lost a few days because of it.

When they finally pulled into Ed O'Neil's mining camp in Shasta County, both girls were very pleased to be there.

Clint climbed down from the wagon, helped Bridget

down, then went around back and helped Bride down as well. When he turned around, he saw Ed O'Neil standing there, watching them. His old friend had his hat in his hand, and an anxious look on his face. He was cleaner than Clint had ever seen him, with his hair—what was left of it— slicked down.

"You old buzzard," Clint said to him. "Why are you so clean? You didn't know when we'd be getting here."

"'Bout a week ago I figured I better start keepin' myself clean," O'Neil said. He looked at the two girls, who appeared to be very shy.

"Bride?" O'Neil said, looking at Bridget.

"Oh, no," Bridget said, "this is Bride, your bride-to-be." She stepped away to stand next to Clint.

O'Neil approached Bride, not daring to touch her, and said, "You're even prettier than I thought you'd be."

"Thank you, Mr. O'Neil," Bride said with a slight curtsy.

"Oh, you're gonna have to start callin' me Ed," O'Neil said. "I mean, if we're to be husband and wife."

"Yes, sir, Mr.—I mean, Ed. This is my sister, Bridget."

"Hello, Miss Bridget," O'Neil said. "I have a cabin ready. It's the one Bride and me will live in when we're married, but for now the two of you can share it."

"Thank you, Mr. O'Neil," Bridget said. "That would be fine."

"Ed," O'Neil said, "you both have to call me Ed."

"Yes, Ed," Bridget said.

"Well," O'Neil said, "I'll show you to the cabin, and my men will get your bags and bring them along."

He and Bride started away, but Bridget stopped and looked at Clint.

"Are we to say good-bye here?" she asked.

"Oh, no," O'Neil said, "Clint will be stayin' for the weddin'—won't ya, Clint?"

"Well," Clint said, "since I brought them all the way, I might as well see the thing through."

O'Neil left and said, "That's fine, because I was figurin' you to be my best man! Come on, ladies."

He ushered the ladies away, leaving Clint standing there, slightly stunned.

FORTY-THREE

O'Neil showed Clint into his office and opened a bottle of whiskey.

"Them ladies is prettier than new gold, ain't they?" he said.

"They are that," Clint said.

They sat at a table and O'Neil poured out two glasses of whiskey.

"I can't thank you enough for this favor, Clint."

"It was my pleasure, Ed."

They both drank, and then O'Neil refilled the glasses. This time they sat back in their chairs and sipped.

"Did you have any trouble?" O'Neil asked.

"Well, Ed," Clint said, "now that you ask, let me tell you about it . . ."

After Clint had related his tale, O'Neil said, "Well, I'll be a sonofabitch! Who the hell would be wantin' to kill my bride-to-be?"

"That's what I was going to ask you," Clint said. "The girls insist they weren't followed by anyone in Ireland. They say they didn't leave any trouble behind. That leaves somebody in this country."

"Well," O'Neil said, "I'm gonna have to think on that for a while, Clint."

"You do that, Ed, because that's an answer I'd like to have."

They finished their drinks and O'Neil said, "I got a place for you to stay, and a bath, if ya want it."

"Oh, I want it. And when's the wedding to be?"

"Tomorrow, if I can get the preacher up here by then. I already sent somebody to fetch him."

"Okay, then," Clint said. "Show me where to stow my things and I'll have that bath."

O'Neil took Clint to a small cabin that wasn't as new as the one the girls were in, and wasn't as clean, but it had been cleaned out some just recently.

"Who am I putting out here, Ed?" Clint asked, looking around.

"Never you mind that, Clint. This place is yours for as long as you stay. Got a big wooden tub right in the back. I'll have it filled with hot water for ya."

"Sounds good."

"I'll send somebody to get you for supper," O'Neil said. "Meanwhile I'll think on that question. I'm sure I can think of whoever wants to hurt me that bad."

Clint nodded and O'Neil took his leave.

Clint went out back later to find the tub steaming. He brought his gun with him. He still wasn't dead sure there wasn't somebody else out there who meant him and the girls—and maybe Ed O'Neil—some harm.

He eased himself into the tub, decided not to soak, but just to get himself washed off and get out. He was too vulnerable sitting in the tub.

He bathed without incident, wrapped a towel around his middle when he got out, and went back into the cabin. There was a light breeze that chilled his wet skin, so he had himself a small shot of whiskey from a bottle O'Neil had left in the cabin.

He was getting dressed when there was a knock on the door. Supper already? he thought. But he took the gun with him anyway.

When he opened the door, Bridget hurried into the cabin and said, "Close the door quickly!"

He did, and turned to face her.

"Hurry," she said, pulling her shirt out of her pants and unbuttoning it. "We don't have much time."

"Bridget—"

"I want to finish what we started months ago, just in case you decide to leave in the morning."

She pulled off the shirt and, naked to the waist, began to undo her pants. When she had them around her ankles, she sat down to take off her boots.

"Bridget, I don't think we should—"

"Clint," she said impatiently. "I am not asking you to marry me. Just to make love to me—now!"

Clint watched her toss away her boots and trousers, then stand before him nude.

Who was he to disappoint her?

FORTY-FOUR

They fell onto the flimsy bed, naked and pressed together. He kissed her neck and shoulders, the freckles on the slopes of her breasts, and then turned his attention to her nipples.

"Down, down," she said, putting her hands on his head. "You know what I've been waiting for ever since that night."

He did know because, truth be told, he was waiting for the same thing—to taste her.

He got down between her legs, nestled in that warm, fragrant bush, and pushed his tongue through the tangle. When he touched her, she gasped and clamped her thighs tightly around his head. He began to lap at her then, and she put her hands on his head and writhed beneath him.

"Oh, yes, oh God, yes . . ." she gasped.

He licked her, kissed, sucked her, shook his head, trying to give her as many different kinds of pleasure he could think of. She lifted her knees up, releasing his head momentarily, her feet up in the air as he continued to administer to her. Finally, her entire body shook and he thought she was going to scream and give them away, only she didn't. The scream seemed to catch in her throat as her entire body went taut, and then she exploded beneath him into a flurry of activity. She wrapped his hair into her fingers, drummed on his back with her heels, and rode the waves until her muscles finally relaxed . . .

That was when he withdrew his face from her crotch, mounted her, and drove his hard cock into her, causing her to gasp again, with her eyes wide.

"Oh . . . my. . . God . . ." she gasped as he began to move in and out of her, slowly at first, then faster and faster until, eyes closed, he was straining to find his own release . . .

"Oh God," she said again, moments later.

"I know," he said. "I'm surprised this bed survived."

She rolled into him and asked anxiously, "You're not going to leave tomorrow, are you?"

"Well, tomorrow is the wedding, so no, not tomorrow. Maybe the next day."

"What about finding out who sent those men after us? Won't that take some time?"

"It might," Clint said. "Ed's giving it some thought now. He should know who hates him that much, though. I think he'll figure it out."

"And then what?"

"And then it'll be up to him."

She moved her hand down over his belly until she was holding his penis in her hand.

"Oh, no," he said, slapping her hand away, "somebody's going to be knocking on my door any minute announcing supper."

"Oh God," she said, springing to her feet. "I can't be here when they do." She started to get dressed.

"Where does Bride think you are?"

"Just taking a walk, giving her time to talk with her groom-to-be and get acquainted."

"So she's going to go through with the wedding?"

"Of course," Bridget said, pulling on her trousers. "We did not come all this way, and go through all we went through—all you went through—not to get married."

"Well," Clint said, "good for Ed."

She rushed to the bed and kissed him quickly.

"I will see you at supper."

She hurried to the door, opened it a crack, peered out, and darted away, closing the door behind her.

Clint sat up, swung his feet to the floor, and took a deep breath. Before he could do anything else, there was a knock on the door.

"Supper, Mr. Adams!" a voice called.

"Be right there!"

FORTY-FIVE

To the delight of Bridget and Bride, supper was thick steaks. Neither girl had grown tired of beef during their trip, and O'Neil was serving the best beef he could find.

They ate in another cabin O'Neil had apparently built for that purpose. Seated at a long wooden table were O'Neil, Bridget, Bride, Clint, and O'Neil's foreman, Bill Tracy. O'Neil's cook was an old chuck wagon cook who found the job with the gold miner when the trail drives petered out.

Ed sat at the head of the table with Clint on his right. Bridget and Bride were seated together at the other end, and it looked to Clint like Bill Tracy was taking an interest in Bridget. And she was returning it. She was glowing, and showing some of the freckles on her chest, which Tracy was drinking in.

"Tracy's a good man," O'Neil said. "Bridget could do worse."

"A lot worse," Clint said. "And she's seen some of the worst on this trip."

O'Neil nodded.

"Speaking of the worst," Clint said, "you figure out who sent those jaspers after us?"

"I can only come up with one name," O'Neil said. "Jock Dewey."

"Who's he?"

"My biggest competitor," O'Neil said. "He's been tryin' to absorb my operation for a couple of years. And he hates me."

"Enough to try and kill two innocent girls?"

"If he thought it would make me easy pickin's, yeah," O'Neil said. "Probably figures I'd fall apart if my bride-to-be got killed."

"So how do you want to play it?"

"Well," O'Neil said, "I can talk to the sheriff and we can go see him. You're welcome to come along, if you want."

"It would be my pleasure."

"Of course, we can't prove it was him," O'Neil said, "and he ain't gonna admit it."

"Maybe he will," Clint said, "if he thinks one if his men gave him up."

"But . . . they both got killed," O'Neil said. "I thought they didn't have time to say a word."

Clint put a thick piece of steak into his mouth, smiled at his friend, and said, "Dewey doesn't know that, does he?"

Watch for

THE LEGEND OF EL DUQUE

377th novel in the exciting GUNSMITH series
from Jove

Coming in May!

GIANT-SIZED ADVENTURE FROM AVENGING ANGEL LONGARM.

BY TABOR EVANS

2006 Giant Edition:

LONGARM AND THE
OUTLAW EMPRESS

2007 Giant Edition:

LONGARM AND
THE GOLDEN EAGLE
SHOOT-OUT

2008 Giant Edition:

LONGARM AND THE
VALLEY OF SKULLS

2009 Giant Edition:

LONGARM AND THE
LONE STAR TRACKDOWN

2010 Giant Edition:

LONGARM AND THE
RAILROAD WAR

2013 Giant Edition:

LONGARM AND
THE AMBUSH AT HOLY
DEFIANCE

penguin.com/actionwesterns

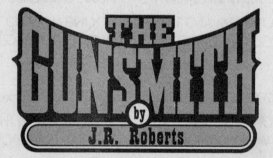